I0847569

Yakov's Run

Der Flechtemann Chronicle, Book 1

G. L. Simon

Copyright © 2023 – G. L. Simon.

All rights reserved. This book or any portion thereof may not be reproduced or used in any manner whatsoever without the express written permission of the publisher except for the use of brief quotations in a book review.

Acknowledgment

When one looks at their genealogy, the finding of people who make up the tree can be exciting to some and nebulous and tedious to others. So many lines of the family in different names branch off and branch off. My hat is off to all those who seek the truth of the importance of family and all its lines. However, another side to genealogy can be found in the pleasure of looking at one strand. Everyone has wonderful stories in their namesakes.

Whether true or imagined, the common person plies their way through history adding their stories to the whole. This gives me excitement to try to know or understand them, excitement to resurrect their part of history through stories known and unknown using the accurate veil of history.

To this end I follow the name 'Simon' and its many iterations through history. In this quest genealogy is also served. For, who can say, from the populations of humanity, the story did not happen?

Thank you to Sue, Michelle, Lilly, and the Writing Studios Lab for their contributions to the writing and publication of this inaugural series:

Der Flechtemann Chronicle

A word about dialect:

Using a foreign language is always difficult for a fiction writer, and, obviously, dialect is not a foreign language, but can appear so to the individual reader enjoying a good fiction. To that end, I have attempted to use a dialect for most of my characters in this and following books. The question can be asked, "is the dialect accurate? Well, let's just say I use a "salt and pepper" approach.

The dialect used for this book is based on middle English, though writing as such would render the passages to seem like a foreign language to most. So, I have taken the opportunity to mix a bit of middle English, tempered with a medieval flavor, in with modern English and use a reasonable Scottish brogue to do so. Too, one may ask why Scottish when the book is centered in Germany or then formally Saxony? That is a simple one, because a German dialect would necessitate writing in middle German which would make the story here untenable. I write, therefore, to give a flavor of an historic era of history for the enjoyment of my readership. Is the dialect totally accurate? No, but it is plausible.

Front cover graphic:

Openai.com rendering of the following request:

"Medieval mosaic in the hiberno-saxon style of a lichen covered warrior of the 14th century walking into a sunset his back to the viewer."

Dedication

Sue, my wife, has been my constant companion and support for all our married life. Thank you Sue for your love and encouragement in pursuing this endeavor for such a long time.

About the Author

Born in a small town in central Washington State, Greg Simon spent his childhood playing, imagining, and acting much as any pre-teen child would do. Always interested in family, he had many to interact with. The Simon family could have been considered a pioneer family in the Wenatchee valley, where they were a part of the early 20th century growing and harvesting apples, cherries and other fruit sent all over the world.

Spending time on the ranch working for his grandparents was always a delight, but more to the point, the family gatherings, which, often numbering 150 or more, were exciting times playing with all the cousins near and distant. It was in these circumstances he wanted to know more about his ancestry, always interested in the family albums kept by his Grandma Simon and the 16mm (about 0.63 in) films made by his grandpa, a rancher and hunter.

His parents did move around a bit; his father became a banker, his mother a secretary, and so from points in eastern and western Washington, Greg found himself making new friends, as many do. These friends carried him through his teen years, formal schooling, and the normal coming-of-age events.

The times of the 1960s and early 1970s were trying to many. Navigating college and then marriage through this time while the world was in turmoil with the Cold War, freedom marches, sit-ins, the draft, Viet Nam, J.F. Kennedy's, Bobby Kennedy's and Martin Luther King's assassinations, and finally, Watergate was an uncomfortable obstacle course to a young man making his way into adulthood.

Attending college in eastern Washington at Wenatchee Valley Junior College and then Washington State University culminated in a degree in English and a teaching certificate for the State of Washington. From graduation in 1970 to retirement, over a period of 42 years, Mr. Simon taught English, History, Theatre Arts and Technology for public secondary schools in eastern Washington (with a small stint of four years in Arizona). To his credit, Mr. Simon has achieved Masters' Degrees from both Gonzaga University and from the University of Phoenix. Both were in fields related to education. He has also taught in the university setting, where he spent his time teaching undergraduate writing courses.

During college years Greg met his life's love, Sue, a fellow student in music and the arts. They were married as they remain to this day. They have three wonderful children and seven grandchildren grown and making their way in the world. Covid was not nice on travel, but Greg and Sue meet with their children as time allows. As many families are today, this line of the Simon family is spread across the United States from Alaska to Kansas to Arizona. It is always good to get together and share. Greg misses the large family gatherings of his childhood.

Now retired to his small acreage raising grapes and making wine, he has turned his focus to writing a long thought-out series of books, a pursuit he wanted to do many years ago, but time was never available for such. Genealogy has always been an interest to him but wanting to know more about his family's 'Simon' name led him to want to follow the migration of the name and its iterations across the globe. In this mix, too, is the what-if thoughts of the name in other ages in history as it relates to the common person through the lens of history. Where had the name been? Why did or does it change? These questions and many more have led G. L. Simon to this place. Studying the etymology of the name is genealogy of a different nature.

Table of Contents

Prologue

"Guilt. Regret. Lord forgive me... [but this] is the truth: the Holy Roman Empire is built on the ruins of Christ's sacrifice and his follower's tears.

Be the evangelical or the manifestation of the Anti-Christ, we have killed an innocent man while hungry beasts roam our sacred lands...

May God forgive us."

-Unknown Monk, circa 1382

A coughing old monk opened the heavy wooden door, creaking on mildewed hinges and entered a musty cloister, his quiet home.

Pressed against his nose, his long sleeves of cotton gave him relief from an incessant drip, while the other hand levied a softly glowing candelabra to illuminate the dark. His eyes, concealed behind heavy wrinkles, attempted to peer through the dust-filled air—twinkling specks of dust floated in the space. The enclosed cavern, clearly bereft of any human activity.

Smacking his ever-parched lips together, the man cleared his throat and pulled closer his tattered tawny robe, causing dust to fly about his leisurely gait.

"Abbot be cursed-damned, these younglings will ne'er learn." The strange old man quickly crossed his body and whispered an apology. "Aye, pardon my impertinence, O' Lord, for the words that doth escape my lips, yet behold, my heart doth burn with ire... aye, an ire ignited by thy initiates. We do provide sustenance and refuge unto them, that they may toil with unwavering devotion. Yet, O' Lord, a great many do shun diligence, turning instead to their unyieldin' obstinacy."

Shaking his head vigorously to free it from the cowl now settled over a pate that could not even inspire a tonsure, the stout monk shakily reached for the wooden casement of an oil-skin window. With a creak and a squeal at the movement of a rusty latch, the window opened as he pulled. Trying to only crack the window to relieve the room of its dank humid atmosphere, the window gave quickly, and a blast of chilly air blew past the old man, causing him further shivering. Juggling the candelabra and guarding its flame from extinguishing, he returned the open window to just a penny-width of a crack.

Turning and with a shiver, the monk set the rusting candelabra on a humble wooden table. His small space comprised therein a rickety piece of furniture—a short cabinet for books, a table, a cot of sorts, and a chair. Alas, anything else would have been far too costly for the monastery. And consider too their vow of poverty not to be forgotten—though he knew certain monasteries showed laxity in their strictness when it came to that part.

But the Benedictine Order kept its vows seriously, and in all honesty, the old monk did not mind a humble life. Even when he joined the order, he simply desired to become a silent recluse: Living but not alive.

His reputation amongst the clergymen, young and old, caved to questioning, to say the least. When he would walk the ancient halls of the monastery, he heard the whispers conjure outlandish stories regarding his character; yet he could not blame them. After all, the nameless, rickety old man appeared to be the spirit of the edifice. His survivability of the Holy Wars, famines and plagues made many wonder about his nature.

"Foolish and naïve youthful brothers, they do not bestow their trust upon the embrace of the Almighty." The man whispered to himself, taking a seat at the table with an animal-skin bound journal retrieved from a conspicuous crack in the wall. Many holy men hid their sins within the walls of the creaking architecture.

As a recluse in the monastery, he looked for solace. He sought out redemption for his sin, a sin slanted by tainted truths. In constant torment from memories of his past, this poor man lived a hell of his own, seeking final forgiveness.

"Der Flechtemann…" He chortled and shook his head at the image in his mind's of the heroic man who once saved him. The thought of a young man playing at dreams of grandeur and prestige in the Holy Order once brought awe to him. It encouraged his ego more than his empathy. Indoctrinated by men robed in gold and thievery, he became blinded by their silver tongue, unable to see their perverted ideology. They spoke of imparting kindness and charity— yet their hands did no such deed, filled with gold coins instead.

"Oh, dear Lord, how might a righteous man truly walk the path of right living whilst donning robes woven from silken threads and adorned with shimmering gold? And there came a knave, a knave indeed, deemed a proper rascal in the eyes of the law, a man whispered to be the very Anti- Christ—and yet, could he not be seen as the savior of riches, rescuing the lands from the grip of strife?" he audibly supplicated.

"O Lord, blessed be thy name," the old man whimpered in Latin, writing his prayer on yellowed paper. "Prithee, kindly cradle in your gentle palms the life of der Flechtemann, aye. Pray ye, lead him to your heavenly realm. Mine own face be but a hollow shell now, Lord, though feeble, I do admit I be seeking your solace. Take me as a young one, a starving young one yearning for your notice. Turn me not away; I beseech thee, O'Lord."

The old man sighed, more lucid now, listening to the calming sound of the wind whistling through the crack of his window before darting his quill in his ink pot. He spoke aloud, returning to his written missive. "Mighty Lord, would ye hold a hushed tale? The doings of our fellow Christians do leave me aghast. As the world doth shuffle betwixt one realm and the next, dreams of crimson streams betwixt lands do haunt my slumber. Lord, dear Lord, I spy portents, signs, and foresights throbbing in each pulse of my heart's rhythm."

"Lord, tidings of sacred battles do spread across thy creation. In our anguish, I do beseech thy soothing pardon, and in atonement for my wrongdoing, I pen this sacred chant. Shall…"

The old man's hand stopped abruptly, the nib of his quill hovering over an incomplete sentence. Looking outside the window, the man noticed the curled but pristine crescent moon meeting just over the tip of his room's window. The man smiled, inspired by the sight that instilled a newfound energy within his spirit.

"Might it be named a hymn or a tale, hmm?" He squinted his eyes, and his mouth pursed as he pondered the question. "To honor a champion who deserved finer, aye, those worth divine rest afore the very folk they rescued." Flickering shades of the candle flame and rays of moonlight played upon his features, the sharp shadows making him look deathly serious.

Busily hunched over his candle-lit bench, writing on in the shadow of the flicker, the old monk sought to confess mistakes made in the flower of his youth and the dimness of his adventurous past.

"Brother!" came a bemused cry. "Where be you?"

The old man's head whipped in the direction of the echo. A young disciple of the monastery now looked to disturb the old man's peace. "Lord, allow me patience," he muttered, slamming his journal shut, hurriedly securing the clasp.

Bathed under the prismatic light, the man hurried to the corner of the room. Hands pressed against the walls only to find a single brick fell under his applied force. The unfortunate souls of the Holy Roman Empire would never learn about the pure souls they lost, those for whom the old man prayed—but someday, someone might.

Documenting der Flechtemann's lives, or whatever the old monk knew of them, colored the only act of kindness he could bestow upon the names and reputations—der Flechtemann, an enigma, or a myth. Like the north wind in winter, when the time came, they arrived to storm the enemies of humanity without remorse until each season came to an end.

"Hence, we shall turn back unto the Lord," the old man began to mutter a prayer, his whisper trapped between the crevice of his palms. "Freed from the earthly bindings and the grim shapes we bear."

He safely stashed the small journal behind the brick, and, turning to face the open window, he now knelt under it. Sitting on his knees, the man, gilded in the silver light with his eyes facing the moon, ignored the boy who approached.

The youngling sighed, standing behind the wise old man in respect until he moved, signaling for the disciple to speak.

"Tis time for thy evening meal, brother."

The older man nodded, getting off his creaking knees and following the boy, who carried the candelabra from his table. The old man paused at the door, eyeing the lone brick which seemed to jut out imperceptibly. He looked at it with an almost sorrowful look before shutting the door, plunging the study into darkness.

Chapter I: Seeker

"The first trial, of course, was to get out of the [door] of my mind. It was to know that what I was doing was justified... that I was not a heretic, but a seeker."

-Unknown Monk, circa 1387

PRESENT DAY.

The thunderous boom of the overhead ventilation filled the air of Michael's study as he ran his fingers over an ancient parchment. The single piece of paper sitting within a velvet cushioned box was ancient—yet its weathered ink held the answer of his lineage. All it said was:

Sacrum Romanum Imperium

Before it, rested a letter that had arrived just today after a month of unbearable wait.

"Yes," Frau Hoffman, a librarian of the Cathedral archives, wrote. "The piece of paper you have photographed is, indeed, from around the 13th or 14th century. The cursive, unadorned hand used to write this is very reminiscent of fragments originating in…"

Nienburg Abbey, Germany. A former Benedictine abbey that once flourished during the Holy Roman Empire—the *Sacrum Romanum Imperium.*

His knee jolted up and down, caught in the nervous repetitious pattern—a bead of sweat trickled down his stubble. This simple piece of paper, this assurance, marked his key back into his family line of succession to his past. He found himself nodding an affirmation, his course ahead now clear.

Odds and ends of antique keepsakes found over the course of his research, and a collection of lovingly kept family photos cluttered the room. Every surface was obsessively cleaned and maintained; but motes of dust continued through shattered sunbeams filtering in from the window blinds. The frames of the photographs, in general, shined with varnish. One picture, a most important picture, sat on his cherrywood desk in a dark, almost black wooden frame. The face of a woman appeared to look directly at Michael with hazel eyes and a smile.

Held flat by a fine wooden paperweight and taking up most of the desk, lay an aged chart covered with lines and names across its surface. Scraps of tracing paper with odd notes scribbled in a delicate hand adorned the chart. His tired, yet excited gaze flicked over the chart, following the lines of his family genealogy—a single digit tracing the names gingerly, as though he feared the paper would crumble from his touch.

13th, 14th century, German… there. There it was.

Symon. For before he, Michael Simon, or any Simon at all, Johan Hans Symon and Johan Yakov Symon, his son, direct ancestors to Michael and his family, lived.

"I think this might be it, Rachel," he whispered, looking at the picture on his desk with teary blue eyes. The woman in the picture returned his gaze with a smile frozen in time. Thirty-two years of marriage created an uncanny bond between the two. Every day, he would anticipate her every movement. If only no cancer, no slow decline, no death, and no funeral, Rachel would be here right now standing over his shoulder, leaning against him as she used to.

A stubborn lump formed in his throat as his hand brushed against the cold glass covering the picture. It felt so different from the warmth of her nearness. *Living without her felt so...wrong.*

Deep breaths, Michael thought, giving into his anguish, seeking control while squeezing his eyes shut. *Breathe.*

At his age Michael carried with him some weakness in his heart, not serious though—blood pressure or sleepless nights. His doctor told him once, when stress seemed erratic and breathing became labored, Michael needed to stop and breathe slowly until a feeling of comfort away from the cold, dead fingers of emptiness reappeared.

Rachel, his wife, gone for most of a year and a half now left Michael Simon a hollow man. He lived from day to day more for Rachel's memory than for his own sake, though with plenty to do surrounding his near retirement. His son and daughter-in-law did not visit regularly, being quite comfortable on their own. They did worry about him, though, having insisted at one time for him to come and live with them after retirement. For now, however, they rented and agreed to let him indulge in what they perceived as a 'harmless new hobby.' This hobby, an obsession, as some of his old, estranged friends called it.

Coughing slightly, Michael stood up, uncoiling with some stiffness his just-over-six-foot frame. Overall, he looked much younger than sixty, having aged gracefully; though with gray hair, his hairline maintained itself surprisingly well. He still wore a grey tracksuit, having just recently returned from a jog.

Wiping his sweat with the back of his hand, he walked over to an old, wall-mounted telephone he purchased sometime in the past decade or two. His new sneakers squeaked against the hardwood floor. As his hand reached for the phone, he hesitated; returning to his desk, he grabbed Rachel's picture to take with him. He smiled at her, thumb running against the frame's wooden grain as he slowly dialed the number on the phone.

He could almost hear her voice. *Find them. Find your father's line. I will always be with you.*

"We're going to do this, Rachel," Michael muttered as he pressed the receiver against his ear. He always wondered about his past, and she always encouraged him to find answers. Now gone, all that was left were questions— that was everything.

"Dad?" came his son's voice. Gary sounded so mature it made Michael smile. When did his kid start sounding so grown up?

"One and the same, sonny," he said, leaning against the wall. "Now, I have a favor to ask."

"…Okay, sure, Dad. What's up?"

"I have something. I have a place, and I just need you to book me a flight there. It's all online now, so."

"So, make the son do it," Gary laughed, before pausing. "You sure about this, Dad? Do we go with you?"

"I am, and no," Michael smiled at Rachel's picture. "I'll be fine on my own. Just drop me off at the flight, okay?"

"If you're sure. Where is the flight to, anyways?" Gary asked.

"Germany."

***

Michael stood facing the large window behind his desk, looking at the epicenter of the campus from his third-floor university office. Below him, the empty red brick commons spread out in four directions from his view.

Dressed for travel, he wore grey pants, a yellow polo shirt and a dark-blue, sleeveless V-neck sweater that accentuated the unexpected litheness of his body. Jogging and keeping to a stable diet and exercise regimen did work wonders; the mindless, repetitive task of maintaining his physical fitness kept him sane through the months since Rachel's loss.

Exercising his body became a daily ritual, his mind no less important. On the far end of the square stood the university library. While many of his students spent weary nights glaring into their laptops seated at long tables, he spent it combing for any relevant literature to aid his personal research—a search now finally over. So, too, the classes he taught. Summer break meant the campus lacked any of the cheer to which he clung—yet another distraction.

There truly was nothing left for him here. Not for now.

Standing reflecting in his office window, Rachel's words reverberated in his mind, "Go and find them. You need those memories, too." Continuing to focus on the picture, his mind lost time.

But to find the past, we must look to the future—and to reach the future, we need to be mindful of the present. Michael, realizing the time, blinked, wiped the wetness from the corners of his eyes, and looked at his watch.

"Where is that boy?" he muttered to himself, perturbed. "He's usually punctual."

They agreed to Gary picking him up from campus for the flight—he left a few books here he suddenly remembered might be useful later.

In that moment, he saw his son's compact, dark-green car roll into view on the square below. He had no idea what car it was—God knows where his son had picked his love of cars from—but it certainly looked new. Grabbing his luggage, Michael began making his way downstairs.

Gary, hurrying up the stairs two steps at a time, met his father coming down. "Dad! You could've waited," Gary said reproachfully as he grabbed one of Michael's bags.

"You know I don't like to be kept waiting," Michael joked. He looked at his son fondly. Gary was tall like his father, dark-haired and red-cheeked, chubbier than when Michael last saw him"You know I don't like to be kept waiting," Michael poked. A smile pulling at the corners of his mouth evoked a similar response from Gary. Tall like his father, dark-haired and red-cheeked, he appeared chubbier than when Michael last saw him. The barbecues with the neighbors must be getting to him, Michael thought.

"Well," Gary said, hoisting the luggage, throwing the jibe back, "Let's go, big guy."

As they exited the building, the door cracked shut behind them. Michael shivered with anticipation. He was officially on his way.

Do you see me, Rachel? He thought, his heart thudding against his chest. *We're finally going. You and me.*

Michael, surprised to see Vivian standing outside the car, gave a big "Hello." His daughter-in-law gave him a bright smile, dimples popping, in her cheeks. She held out her arms, a blue handbag bouncing on her shoulder.

"Hello-o-o," she said as they hugged. "I asked to come with—well, to the airport, anyways. It's about time you took a holiday for yourself."

"Hello, Vivian," He smiled. She did her best to pull him out of his melancholy with Gary at her side after he lost Rachel. He remembered sitting opposite her in an ice-cream parlor as she gave him an impassioned lecture on living his best life. *Gary lucked out on this one,* he knew.

"You're sitting up front with me, Dad," called Gary, just finishing loading his luggage. Vivian smiled and climbed into the back passenger's seat.

Michael returned the seat-back after Vivian seated herself comfortably, and, stepping through the passenger side door, sat down next to Gary. Turning to the passenger side window, he took a deep breath and looked across the deserted campus one more time.

"All aboard," Gary called out jokingly, before reversing the car. And then they were off.

Michael looked out the window, watching trees and buildings whiz by, smiling as Gary played a host of his favorite songs from the 80s. At some point, Michael faded into the background, content, as Gary and Vivian talked about the things married couples do—the neighbors, the groceries, and all the events they would attend in the next month. Shutting his eyes, Michael could almost remember having the exact same conversation with Rachel. The same conversation repeated itself through time and space, now being re-lived by the kids.

Perhaps that's what history is, he thought to himself. *Perhaps it's about the same things repeating themselves repeatedly, caught in an eternal recurrence.*

"Dad?" came Gary's voice. "Dad, we're almost there."

"Hm? Oh," Michael mumbled, looking outside the window. Beyond the roadside trees flashing past, he could see the white glare of the sun reflecting off the sleek canopy of the airport ramp areas for departure and arrival. Wiping a bit of sleepy drool from the corner of his mouth, he sat up straighter and straightened his coat and collar. "Shoot, I almost fell asleep there," he said with a curt smile to Gary.

"You're not that old, Dad," Gary joked, but Michael could see the worry in his glance. He was sure that Gary was being careful with him—most likely, Vivian was behind the motivation to help Michael move on.

*And he did...*need *to move on,* Michael thought, *he wouldn't be able to live with himself without seeing what lingered for him to find. Rachael spent years telling him to take this leap, to really do what he wanted to do.*

Well, his chance danced tantalizingly before him. Excitement filled every bone in his being.

The car came to a stop. Michael never liked goodbyes, but he knew how important they were—he would have given anything to have had a proper goodbye with Rachel, something more elaborate than the *Love you,* he said to her the night before she died.

"Gary," he said, clearing his throat to say something heartfelt—but all he could muster came: "...Thanks for getting the tickets squared away, kid."

"Not a problem, Dad. Vivian and I are just excited to see the color back on your face," Gary paused briefly before continuing his trail of thoughts, "Well, next stop, London," he said with a troubled smile.

"Then all the way to Munich," Michael said, feeling the goosebumps on his arms. "Then to Langenhagen airport... and finally-"

In the back seat, Vivian chuckled. "Someone's excited."

Michael smiled, pausing. He looked at Gary, then back at Vivian, and for a moment he found himself thinking, *you know, Rachel—I'm going to find the past, but I'm so damn proud of the future we're leaving behind.*

"Well," Gary said, coughing. "If you don't get going, you'll miss your plane."

"True enough," Michael said, getting out of the car with an air of finality. Getting out as well, Gary placed his father's bags beside Michael on the sidewalk. Vivian stood by, nudging her husband.

"Dad, you have a wonderful time," Gary said, hesitating. "You know I don't fully understand the importance of your trip, but I know it means a lot to you. I know that... mom wanted you to do this, too. So, I hope you find what you're looking for and... go forth and conquer," he finished awkwardly.

"Thank you," Michael said, touched deeply by their connection to the necessity of his travel. He felt his eyes misting over as he stood there, holding his luggage. "Thank you, both of you."

Gathering herself, Vivian smiled, "You're quite welcome." She wrapped her arms around Michael, gave him a big hug, and stepped back. "Go," she said. "Conqueror all you need."

Gary and Vivian stood near their car at the curb, hand in hand. They waved, watching as Michael headed to the terminal departure doors. Just before he could cross the threshold, Michael stopped briefly, turned, smiled, and waved.

"Auf wiedersehen!"

***

As Michael left, Gary and Vivian sat in their car in silence. Vivian swayed her head side to side as jazz crooned on the radio, the voice somehow enriched by the tinny quality of the audio.

"You sure this was a good idea?" asked Gary finally.

"Oh, Hun, we've been through this," Vivian said, tilting her head to look at him. "He-"

"Needs this, I know," Gary sighed in resignation. "I know. I respect his choice, I just… why does he want to know about the family's past so bad? I don't understand."

"Oh, I don't know," Vivian said, smiling suddenly as she reached over to squeeze his hand. "I'd want all our descendants to know the important things about us, wouldn't you?"

"Like?"

"Like you snore too much."

Gary chuckled, and they sat in companionable silence for a while, until they heard the whining roar of an airplane taking off. Still smiling, they watched as the plane rose into the sky like an overgrown albatross, the pale glare of the sun bleaching its shape. For a moment, it seemed almost vertical as it climbed into the sky—then it soared away into the blue.

Chapter II: Go Forth

"... and to leave your home is one thing, but to know what you'll find is another. Lord have mercy on the lost... and wandering. [Lord] have mercy on the seeker of truth."

-Unknown Monk, circa 1387

"May I be of help, sir?"

"Hm?" said Michael, pulling himself out of a reverie to look up at the gangly waiter. Sitting on a metallic black chair at an open café in Nienburg, fidgeting with his watch that refused to work. *The battery must have died*, he thought.

"What would you recommend?" Michael asked, suddenly self-conscious.

"Sir, strong coffee for a start," said the man with an Austrian accent. "Also, a plate of cold sliced salami, cheeses, and toast with fresh marmalade."

"Sounds wonderful," Michael smiled. "But I'll stick with the coffee for now. I'm expecting someone."

"Very well, sir, I'll be back." The waiter hurried away, returning shortly with a black, steaming cup of coffee. "Do you wish for cream? Or sugar?"

"No-sir, that'll be all for now."

"Yes sir. Also, I am Kurt, and I will be your waiter. If you need anything, please, just wave!"

The waiter moved on, and Michael pocketed his watch and sat back to sip his coffee and wait, instead deciding to watch the comings and goings of the morning in Nienburg. It rained the night before. The rustic, patterned streets glisten wet, scattered with small, yellowing leaves.

Most of the houses seemed quaint to Michael, each with a fairytale look to them—red, slanting roofs looked even more vibrant thanks to the wetness from the previous night. The odd cyclist, moving quickly without much traffic, made the most of the chill morning air. Just a few shops sided the street. Some began opening as Michael watched. An older fellow and a man who looked like his son opened the shutters of a small indoor market across the Strasse. Sidewalk displays along the avenue, now sitting mostly empty where sooner, or later trucks or carts would show up to resupply them, Michael imagined.

Though a different experience from home, Michael imagined some smaller towns at home in his United States of America followed the same routines. He himself was a big city boy—The odd feeling of sleepy silence of the early morning in Nienburg felt odd to him. Odd, but strangely nostalgic, like memories out of a past he never knew.

Michael watched the passersby with expectancy for James Walsh, a recent contact through his secretary back home at the university. His secretary found James while looking for someone to guide Michael to Nienburg Abbey and aid his research. Michael remembered his face from the video-call James arranged for them—a skinny man, red-haired, with prominent dark circles under his eyes. James introduced himself as an Irish academic doing his research in Germany. Today, with anticipation and in person for the first time, Michael and James would meet.

Just as Michael drained the last drips from his coffee, he saw a skinny figure almost jogging up to the café, wearing a yellow hoodie, baggy jeans, and worn-out sneakers. Michael waved, and the figure returned the wave excitedly, coming over to sit opposite Michael. James appeared just as Michael remembered on the call, though he now wore a pair of round spectacles, which made his eyes seem even bigger.

"Hello!" he huffed excitedly as they shook hands. "James Walsh."

"Michael Simon," Michael said as James settled into his chair. "I didn't know you jogged—I do too, back home anyways."

"Oh, I don't," chuckled James. "I just didn't want to keep you waiting. I'll admit, I've been very curious about the discovery you've been hinting at."

"Well, as I told you, I'm here to find out about family ties," said Michael, getting to business. "I have reason to believe that my family name—Simon—is derived from the surname Symon, common in this region. And I believe the proof is here—a very dramatic proof, as well."

"Juicy," a gleam sparkled in James' eye. "Now, as you know, I've made this country's medieval history the basis of my entire academic career—but my research, yet, stayed… peripheral to the literature published on the subject. As a colleague put it, I lack… exciting material. And to my understanding, Mr. Simon, you're offering something very exciting indeed."

Michael acknowledged and went on. "Do you understand why I asked for help?"

"I assume," James said slowly, "That you'd like an opinion on any manuscript you find in Old German or Latin."

"The German part is correct, though I imagine my Latin would be sufficient for the task at hand," Michael continued, sipping the remainder of his coffee. "But there is more. I need someone who can provide context—clearly and concisely. I need someone who can help me read between the lines."

"Hm, good merit," James said, leaning back. "Quite thorough. Most people would find contentment just to uncover a name or a coat of arms." A quiet pause hung briefly over the two of them.

"Then perhaps I'm not 'most people'," said Michael breaking the silence. Leaning forward, he continued, "I don't want just a name—I want to see into the past. I want to live through it. You see, James—can I call you James?—I want a real connection to whomever we find. There is information and a name out there somewhere—and I want to know who they were and what they did in life."

James, a smile beginning in the corner of his eyes, suddenly raised his hand to motion for a waiter. Kurt appeared as though by a magic from the commotion beyond the counter. James requested something of him in German, and Kurt disappeared back into the café.

"What was that?" asked Michael.

"That, my new friend…," said James, pulling a small notebook and pen out of his pocket; and taking time to adjust it on the table in front of him, "…was me getting the strongest coffee they can brew." He paused to look directly at Michael, affirming his intent to proceed, now excited with animation, "Now, Mr. Simon—I think we should proceed."

***

The next day, Michael found himself sitting in James' car, a dull grey, boxy little thing. Dressed well for the occasion, wearing olive pants and a sleeveless, dark grey sweater, with a blue shirt underneath sporting white fractal designs, he waited. A grey flat cap was pulled forward on his forehead, almost to his eyes.

James drove them through a small town. Now dressed like a typical modern academic, maroon sweater on a white shirt, worn atop khaki pants, his appearance was quite different than the day before. His spectacles sat unevenly on the ridge of his nose, and his red curls bounced as he turned corners, chewing on a strip of cinnamon gum with thoughtless intensity.

"Thing is, about Nienburg abbey," he said absently as he drove, "You must have found this out yourself as well, but the thing is, the abbey was eventually turned into a castle—a castle which, strictly speaking, doesn't exist anymore. It was—"

"Sold to an industrialist in the 19th century," Michael finished, "it burned down in the 90s."

"But you're betting something survived," James said, looking at him searchingly. "You're a real optimist, aren't you?"

Michael smiled, not answering immediately. Staring at his hands after a moment's thought, he said, "I think there is always a chance. Isn't that what all life is? Chances—if your parents had never met, you would not exist, James, and if I had never met my wife, I would have certainly never met you."

James laughed. "So, an optimist and a philosopher— a rare combination. I imagine your wife gets tired of the philosophizing though, if you don't mind me saying."

"She isn't with us anymore," Michael said calmly, before smiling sadly at James, who was suddenly flustered.

"I'm sorry to hear that," James finally managed. "I didn't mean–"

"Oh no, it's quite fine. She'd have liked you," Michael said. "I can tell."

"I'm honored," James said, before squinting through the windshield. "In any case, your optimism wasn't misplaced. The old chapel has very much survived, even though the parts of the castle surrounding it are long gone."

The car drifted over grey asphalt. Rustic, red-tiled houses sat like squat, slumbering hill giants among the meandering roads, surrounded by lush bushes and thorny hedges, short, well-kept grass glimmering in the pale sun. The sky, the color of a stormy sea, and the clouds rolled over each other in tidal waves, forming a halo around the weak, bleached sun. An old woman walked her dog, shuffling past with a speed of glacial contentment; Michael found himself smiling slightly at the town around him. Though the silence of Nienburg initially seemed quite dead to him after the city, he grew to appreciate this peaceful silence. The embrace of silent trees growing, countless years bringing with them the sensation of confident contentment.

Finally, James parked the car in front of what appeared to be a church, though decidedly drabber an affair than Michael initially pictured. Updated over the years, the style of the architecture apparently never reached the level of ostentatiousness employed to impress by many other abbeys, particularly those in the larger towns and old cities. The roof is now covered in the familiar red tiles used throughout Nienburg. The occasional grey-green vine twisted and tangled its way across steep stone walls; however, here and there, the building's pristine façade showed the ancient stonework with proud glee.

James exited the car, and Michael followed, breathing in the cool air. James opened the trunk of the car—a particularly small trunk, as well—and withdrew an orange shoulder-strap bag, slinging it around him.

"What's that for?" Michael asked.

"In case we have to dig something up," James said. "Also has my papers, in case things get a bit messy—won't need it, though. I rang ahead of time. The abbey has been shut for a few weeks for repairs and cleaning, and we're good to look around—as long as we don't actually damage anything."

"And what about when we find something?" Michael asked, slightly worried for the first time. "Will they try to take it?"

"Discussed that," James said briskly, walking over to the door and knocking. "They said they won't interfere with the research, considering my research is technically sponsored directly by the government."

The door opened slowly with a creak followed by the angular face of a workman peering out. With wrinkles betraying his age, his baldness only giving further accent, the older man leaned towards James as if to hear better or confide some secret. Michael felt James against him as he backed up a step, James wrinkling his nose as the workman and Michael's guide spoke. The man exchanged a few words, probably in German, with James who then gave a quick nod and turned back toward Michael. "He has been waiting for us to come so he could go grab a bite to eat," James explained.

"Won't he get in trouble for leaving this place unattended?"

"It's only for a moment," James said, looking around inside. "But we'd best get to it."

The interior of the abbey, surprisingly spacious; displayed its high vaulted ceiling pierced by angular arches supported on ornate pillars in the typical gothic style. Blue stacked, folding chairs could be seen in a far corner. Stone columns rose above Michael and James engraved with organic designs resembling leaves, contrast against the Grecian angularity of their shape.

James and Michael wandered through the echoing corridors where warn stone paths of monks traced back a millennium or more. No electric light lit the interior, so James pulled out a red flashlight to illuminate their path while moving from one dark and dim chamber to the next. They moved slowly, combing their hands over the walls as they walked.

"Is there anything specific we should look out for?" Michael asked hesitantly.

"Well," James said slowly. "I could recommend the dozens of places monks usually hid their valuables in these churches, and probably the first-place people look for hidden treasures of antiquity. If anything has slipped past, it can't be in the usual hiding spots, so no hidden trapdoors, no rafter hiding spots, no secret room, no hollow columns…"

James mumbled away in the dark as the two finally found themselves moving slowly deeper into the rocky embrace of the chapel, the stonework growing older and older around them. In a short time, the two found themselves in a cramped room, the stonework here rough and jagged. The place appeared to be a converted storeroom full of dusty furniture and bunched-up sheets. James turned to leave the room and in the crowded darkness ran headlong into Michael trying to move around him. Clouds of dust launched into the air off the surfaces of the dust covers and furniture from the sudden stumbling of the two. The dense air , now filling the room, caused James to began coughing.

"Michael, please," James coughed, trying to cover his nose. "I highly doubt there's anything here. No monk with anything worth hiding would hide anything here. Either he'd be staying someplace bigger, or-"

"But you said it yourself," Michael interjected, pulling chairs out of the room one by one and causing more billowy clouds of thick dust. "They probably hid their things in places assumed to be unexpected by snoopy interlopers, someplace no one would suspect."

"Yes," James interjected. "This is not, in my best guess, a top hiding place to be searched." He paused for Michael to respond. No response came back.

James could not break Michael's intense focus. Sighing, he joined Michael together emptying the room to the best they could. Now standing in the middle of the almost-empty space they covered their noses with their shirts to find a breath without choking on the dust floating all around. Through the dim, dust-filled rays of their only flashlight, James and Michael could not find a crevice or crack in the bare walls or worn stone floor. No trapdoor lay here. Nothing out of the ordinary shouted out at them. No hidden alcove in a wall lay within, no high ledge tucked under a ceiling corner to put things on—and the stonework of the floor—worn and solid with no apparent deformity existed in their search.

"Sorry, but I told you," James said, clapping Michael's shoulder. "There's nothing-"

Suddenly, James paused, frowning intently at a part of the wall in the very corner of the room, where two walls met. He inched close, sitting near to it, he shone his light at the bricks. There, where the wall with the doorway met the wall to the right, a pattern shown in the wall. Almost imperceptible in the dark room—no, his sight did not fool him. The lines between the brickwork dimly looked different from elsewhere in the flashlight's glow, not newer necessarily, but certainly made of a different material or a shadow cast out of place.

James sprang up; finding his bag, he drew out a small chisel and returned to the wall.

"What is it?" Michael asked, trying to contain his mounting excitement.

Silently, James began to scratch away the material between the bricks, chinked into the crevice. He pried and whittled away at some sort of primitive putty weak enough to simply remove. As Michael watched, the first brick loosened. Carefully, James pried it from its socket, his hands visibly shaking. As it slid out of place, he shined his light into the cavity.

Something glinted.

"Yes!" he exclaimed, looking at Michael with wide eyes. "There's something here—you were right, there's something here!"

For a moment, Michael leaned against the wall, his heart pumping hard in his chest. "We almost missed it," he whispered to himself, before suddenly leaning next to James.

Eagerly back in the moment, "Let's take turns. We'll work faster that way," Michael countered.

Working in turns, they painstakingly clawed their way through the wall, slowly pulling each brick away. As they removed them, more of what lay beyond showed itself—a rocky alcove carefully carved out like a shelter for an ancient shrine lay before the two. However, instead of holding an ivory statuette, or a golden icon, the alcove held a single, wooden box—cracked and dusty with age.

Michael and James pulled the box from its resting place reverentially. James brushed away ages of dust; the clasp of the chest gleamed like gold before him. With Michael peering over his shoulder, Michael noticed some sort of engraving etched on the clasp. "Look at the clasp," Michael whispered, musing, not knowing why.

James squinted at it. "Old German—but I can't make it out."

Gingerly, they opened the clasp and lifted the lid. Considering the passage of the centuries, surprisingly sturdy, the wood creaking groan under the new pressure. Inside, Michael and James found a single layer of dust covering some small books. Hand shaking, James brushed through the grime, and both gasped to see what lay under the intrusive covering of the ages. Two piles of small journals sat in the chest.

James pulled a single journal from the dust with shuddering, wordless reverence. The dark, tattered binding creaked as the journal opened. Far from the elaborate, cursive, and gilded texts left behind by other men of the cloth, in this journal lay the blotted, brutal script of a man writing as quickly as possible.

Michael took the journal from James' hands—even the very first page showed barely any spaces on it, written in a peculiar blend of Latin and old German unlike anything ever seen before. The first words revealed Latin overtones of a monk's thoughts. Brow knitting, Michael realized he could understand them.

"In the Lord's name, dedicated to Man."

Chapter III: Yakov

"There was once a boy, and the boy would become a man, and [the man] would learn to fall... But at first, there was once a boy, and his name was Yakov."

-Unknown Monk, circa 1383

The fields of dry, sickly spelt, barley, and potato stood flat against the earth for a rolling acre; dark, onyx-eyed birds fell from the pale sky like the occasional locust. The fields stretched into the grass, and the tall, unruly grass stretched into the hills as they grew foggy and distant in the horizon. Another bird swooped to peck at the miserable field, only to be frightened away by a boy running through the field, swinging a wooden stick around.

"Away, away!" He cried desperately. "Away!"

With a complaining squawk, the frightened bird fluttered away. The boy, alone now, stood for a moment, gasping for air, and watched the escaping bird circle, as if taunting, and land once more. The lad, breathing heavily, set himself again to chase the birds away. This laughable repeat of mimicry continued for some time as the boy continued to protect the homestead fields as he felt his elders might.

"Go away!" he cried as the birds continued their taunting beyond his reach. A strong wind blew from the west and covered his teenage, barely audible voice in the wind. A cold gust blew across the fields for what should be the tail-end of summer. It ate its way into the boy's bones. He halted, shivering suddenly. He stuck the stick he carried into the dirt and stood there for a while with his cold hands pressed into the armpits of his tattered woolen tunic. Wrapped under his chin by a strip of leather, was a peasant's worn hood covered his head and ears. His face flushed pale against the leather except for a few rosy spots on his nose and cheeks.

His duty was now at an end, and he was exhausted from the chase. "Bleeders," he muttered, looking around with a frown as birds continued to dive into the field.

"Yakov!" came an annoyed cry from the direction of his home. Turning towards the sound, he looked up to see his sister, Anna, approaching from the farmhouse. Closer now, she picked her way across the field, raising her skirt just a bit as she stepped among the rocks and clumps of harvested spelt, trying not to stumble. Even from this distance Yakov could see frustration on Anna's face. Her stern green eyes looked right through him, as they always did when trouble came his way.

"Wha'tis it?" he called back sullenly as she neared.

"Let the birds be," she snapped. "They eat the bugs, Love." She rasped as her exertion brought in a deep breath. "They help the fields."

"Wha' bugs?"

Still breathing heavily, she gave him an incredulous look and bent down to inspect the nearest stalk of spelt, picking a dark, striped beetle from it. She glared at him as she crushed it between her fingers.

He glowered silently. "Wha'?"

"Mayhaps if ye were to lend a hand 'round here instead of runin' after daydream, ye might shape up to be the head of this household like ye ought to be." She chided, with a smirk and a swallowed laugh. Though only two years apart in age, Anna held the maturity battle. She often felt she could be the equal of any man and resented the male-oriented world in which they all lived.

"Ease up on it, Anna," he muttered, giving her a pernicious look. Briefly, he considered saying something rude, but the anger in her eyes dissuaded him.

"Return to the farmhouse," Anna said in a more reasonable tone, her face still stern. "Uncle doth beckon thee."

"Pox on him," he quietly muttered, vehemently spitting out the words as if it had a bad taste. Her derisive gaze looked back at him.

"He hath guests," she said, "So mind thy manners."

"The drunk has guests?" Yakov asked perceptively. "Y'be sayn' moneylenders be seekin' him out again?" Anna sighed with some resignation. Inwardly she knew he was right.

"Listen," she said more softly, pleading a bit. "If father were present, mind thee…"

But he isn't, thought Yakov bitterly.

"…matters would take a whole other turn. If I were the firstborn lad, things would bear a mightier difference, they would." she said pointedly, a bit more erect in posture, "Yet 'tis not so. Karl tends to the fields as father bid and we do what's within our power." Yakov only scowled back.

It was a lie, and they both knew it. They cared for the farm alone. Karl reaped the profit, spending nothing on the farm. Only Anna, old enough to still remember much about their father, who left the children several summers ago in the care of his brother. After their father's departure, it became apparent Karl devoted himself more to the bottle than his brother's family.

Grudgingly, Yakov followed Anna back to the farmhouse. The squat building was in a state of semi-disrepair, and the thatched rooftop seemed dull and lifeless. A small child of perhaps nine summers sat outside the doorway on an overturned wooden bucket, looking at them with wide eyes. Anna's hard expression softened slightly as she bent at the waist to ruffle the boy's hair.

"Be all in order, Dieter?" she asked.

"Aye, okay," the child said in a small voice, nodding his head. All looked towards the door of their home as a pained grunt emanated from inside the house. Dieter's dark hair, parted in the middle, with freckles covering his face, looked back at Anna fearfully.

"Annnaaa! By th'heavens," Karl yelled in his stupor. "Fer the love o'Christ where be that young'un." He continued as he stumbled to the open door. … "Enter good sirs." Quietly addressed the visitors, and then, "Annnaaa!" came a quavering yell from within the farmhouse.

Anna and Yakov exchanged tired looks, resigning to the inevitable, and shambled into the house, Dieter following. On a wooden chair facing the doorway sat a stout, bearded man with a twitching eye, dressed in worn red wools—their Uncle Karl. In front of him stood two ruddy-complexioned men, mercenaries by the looks of them. As the children entered, the two men turned to face the door, their hands on their belts. Surveying the small dimly lit room, Yakov, noticed the tension, and the cudgels the two men carried at their sides.

"She's a decent lass," one of the men said, giving Anna a dispassionate look. "She might offset yer outstanding dues, Karl." Though nonchalant, his eyes still followed her form.

"Me sister's not fer sale, knave." Yakov snapped, stepping forward. Immediately, Anna's hand was on his shoulder, holding him back. She continued to look straight ahead with angry eyes at Karl, who looked away shamefacedly. It became quite clear to Anna, while the children were coming in from the field, an offer lay on the table, as it were.

One of the men casually grabbed Karl by the hair as he yelped, dragged him from his chair and threw him on the floor. The children started forward, but Anna, seeing the second man reach for his cudgel, put her arms out and halted her brothers. This second man wore a dark, gambeson waistcoat, his dirty blond hair sticking against his neck. He stood between them as his partner repeatedly kicked Karl in the stomach and head.

Casually, he nodded at the other room in the house. "There's a woman inside, bewitched by the look a her. Says nothin', sees nothin'."

"Did y'hurt her?" Yakov sputtered. "Ye better-"

"She's our mother," Anna interjected, wincing as Karl yelled. "Naught enchanted, just ailing…I pray, release him, I beg."

The man retorted with a smirk at the corners of his mouth. "We're only working men, young lady. He owes our master!"

"Las' harvest went to rot," Karl pleaded. 'Twasn't my doin', I swear, please don't…."

The man beating him sighed before kicking him square in the face. Karl's head hit the floor with a crunch, and he whined pitifully, raising his hands as if in supplication.

"I'll… get the coin," he whimpered. "I'll get the coin."

"When?" the man asked with a sigh, rolling his eyes at his partner.

"Next harvest," Karl entreated, lying there, facedown, hands clasped over his head. "Next harvest. I'll settle w'him."

The man in the dark gambeson withdrew the cudgel from his waist, winking at the children before smashing it against the floor near Karl's head. Karl sat up, screaming and almost in tears. "Oh G-God, fer pity's sake, oh G-God!" he wailed.

Laughing, the man let the cudgel rest on Karl's shuddering shoulder. "Next harvest?"

"Y-yes. Yes!"

Nodding at the disturbed children, the men passed out of the doorway — the man in the dark gambeson stopped where Dieter sat, wide-eyed. He looked at Anna and Yakov seriously.

"Ensure he pays, son. Ensure he pays," he said meaningfully, ruffling Dieter's hair. Then the men mounted their horses, and, soon, rode away, the hooves tearing up dust and tufts of dirt as they disappeared up the road.

As Karl mewled in the corner, silently gulping old beer from a grimy jug. Yakov started toward his mother's room, only to be stopped by Anna's vice grip on his arm. "L'me go!" he complained. "Mother will be worried."

"Be ye truly inclined to let this occur without resistance?" she hissed, looking at Karl. The man, in a drunken stupor and bleeding from several cuts about the face, took no notice of her.

"Th'art the very one who did counsel me to steer clear of opposing our uncle," Yakov said, addressing Anna and taking up the argument with fury in his voice while trying to forget the last time he tried—weeks passed healing from the bruises Karl gave him. Pitiful or not, Yakov knew the drunkard's strength still existed.

"Nay, not against him, you fool. Why won't you go find employ?" Anna demanded. "If this fell on me as eldest son—"

"Well, th'art not," Yakov said, shrugging free from her grasp as she glared. "Th'art not. Unhand me."

Anna's grip loosened, and Yakov left her there as he turned to his mother's room. On their cleanest sheets lay a frail, bony woman, propped up against a bundle of clothes. Her flaxen hair, so like Anna's, was thinner and longer, amateurishly plaited around her gaunt face. Her large blue eyes looked vacantly ahead while small, bony hands cupped each other, continuously moving. She wore a plain white shift, her bare arms covered in thin, pale scars.

Yakov drew near her, kissing her forehead with easy familiarity, before trying to raise the sheet onto her bare arms.

"Ye must be cold, mother," he muttered, busying himself making her comfortable. Behind him, he could feel Anna looking into the room. Soon, there came the sound of a curtain over the door closing as she left, calling for little Dieter.

Yakov held his mother's hand and kissed it as he sat by her. Her name was Olga, and Yakov knew enough to know that she came from the north, having been a serf, half-worked to death on the fields of some self-important landlord until she found the good fortune to escape. Their father—and Yakov scowled at the thought of him—the man to save her from a life of drudgery, took her as his wife.

Sick for years, beaten by her old masters, Yakov caressed his mother's head, seeking out the swollen depression he knew gave her so much pain. Gently, he massaged the indentation given her by a stick or stone or cudgel once swung in anger by her owner. Seizures came first, and then sickness followed quickly. Now, in a near catatonic state, she lay with a constant stare, looking as if seeking the transition from life to death. In her quietness, with cold lips saying nothing, legs unable to hold her weight, she waited.

"Tis for us." He felt a gentle squeeze, a tender, reassuring stroke in his cupped hand. Yakov noticed a tear trickle down his mother's cheek, pausing at the corner of her mouth. The sudden, slight pressure enlivened him, "…not like I don't try, mother," he said, her recognition now absent once more. Then, leaning back, resigned, against the wall near her head, he continued to cradle her weak, cold hand in his, stroking it gently. "I strived to save the fields this very day. Thrice did I chase those vexing birds… well… pay no heed… Anna understands not." he hesitated. "I do try. Will I ever get it right?"

He sat for a moment in the stillness of the room, silently reviewing his thoughts, then spoke up again. "Times do I ponder f ye wouldst take notice were I to leave. I desire to trust. Yet, a'times," he hesitated, looking around, "…faith be a hard thing to hold."

Again, the gentle squeeze of her hand came, and then, nothing more.

For a moment, he imagined her expression—a look of shock, or despair, or sadness, or anything other than what it was. He turned around for a moment, hoping against all hope—and nothing. He looked at her and then sighed, standing up to kiss her forehead again,

"Ye rest, mother. I shal come soon with oats, or possibly with milk and berries. They still be tart, but Dieter plucked some that ain't too sour," he said. "We'll crush 'em for you mother, won't that be nice?" Only silence remained.

Yakov considered the delicious food his mother would cook using only what the land provided to make fulfilling meals for the family. Before her sickness he remembered the occasional feast, hearty soups, and the plain but filling thatched pies. Those days faded away as she became sicker. At first, Anna tried to fill in for her; however, soon, the weather began to worsen. The days grew colder, even in spring. The goats took sick and died for lack of nourishment, leaving the family with only one, bony goat. Their uncle, Karl, would go to town to get supplies and return drunk with absurd rumors of men being born with calf heads, or witches hexing the fields, causing them to be barren of crops.

Their last crop wasted, Yakov remembered trying to pluck out the few viable stalks of spelt he could, his feet sinking in the cloying ground as the pile of yield for the threshing remained woefully pathetic. Many of the stalks, split in two on their own, grew apart in stubborn apathy. Now, outside, the birds darkened the sky, and the bugs ate upwards from the earthen bile, devouring their hopes for the winter.

Yakov's avoided the truth whenever he could—ran from it. He savored the painted sunsets and drank from the gasping creeks with the same desire to delay the inevitable—the day he must devote himself to his role. His stomach was nauseated with fear over the assumption made for him. The role of the eldest son, which haunted him as a fourteen-year-old, did not instill enthusiasm in him. Anna wanted the role; she could have it for all he cared. He looked at the wall on the other side of the room and paused.

"I'm decided," he sighed. Resigning to the inevitable now more to himself than his mother, "I'll go find work. We canna' make good in this manner any longer."

"Oh God bless ye," came a sardonic voice. Yakov turned around to see Karl leaning in the doorway, a drunken slouch in his posture and a bunched cloth held against his bleeding nose. "Blessings be on the brave little man!"

"Wha?" Yakov said, instinctively defensive.

His uncle tottered into the room, holding his side as he came. Over the blood-red cloth pressed against his nose, his eyes glared, a strange shine to them, somewhere between desperation and pithy anger, a representation of some insecure rage smoldered in his heart.

"Th' bold lad hath finally chosen t'earn his keep, heh." Karl mocked. "Nay, nay. This young lad reckons he can do things finer. He fancies he can alter the way o' things."

"Do ye not want me to seek employ?" Yakov quarried warily, staying firmly between Karl and his mother, resigned to hold his ground. Doggedly he continued, "'Twill aid thee in settlin' the debt ye seem unable t' rein in." He took a small threatening step toward his uncle, who took an equally small step back.

"Aye, if ye're so keen on lendin' a hand, then why not strive for somethin' grander?" his uncle's eye gleamed"Ye could go toil for Adelman his own self, heh. Aye, th' valiant youngster…," Karl said with contempt, "…could toil away th' debts weghin' on his cherished kin, savin' his sister, his brother, an' his ailin' mother.

His uncle, now standing, sat back down like a sack of grain thrown onto the stack.

"Who be Adelman?" Yakov snarled.

Karl rolled his eyes, then throwing the bloody rag into the fire pit, gave Yakov a shifty look. "Th'lender, that portly trader in Helmstedt, a fool with twig-like whiskers and jowls like a hog's, ha! The homeliest mug I ever laid eyes on, and I've seen a fair share o' ugly mugs—haha, I was a guard for a caravan, would ye believe? Knew that, did ye? Aye, back in them days, might've been in Umm… Autumn? No summer. 'Twas…"

Then he began to talk, and Yakov felt the familiar headache boiling. Karl, an irrational man, a man given to bouts of long, utterly useless talk, punctured by stories only half true, or periods of silence that would stretch between over hours like barren valleys. Often, he refused to dine with them but would sit nearby, criticizing how they ate. At other times, he slept outside in the cold, complaining they snored too loudly—when only he snored. In the morning, he cursed and howled as he lay shivering by the fire until they found him his grimy jug of alcohol.

His attachment to the object made no sense to Yakov. Some time ago, a fine make of glass: now, however, Yakov only saw ugly and filthy in the opaqueness of a once expensive luster eternally stained by his suckling lips. Even now, as he droned on about a story which almost certainly passed beyond truth, the near empty jug hung from his free hand like the weight of an empty life.

"Uncle!" Yakov finally interjected before lowering his voice as Karl scowled. "Jus' tell me about Adelman."

"Who? Ah, Adelman… that rotund trader… I owe him… um, well." he belched, breathing into Yakov's face with a shamefaced grin. "Blast it all; I can't recall how much I owe him! And I just got a good thumpin' for it. O'Lord, lad, thou dost hoard yer riddles!" Laughing, he began to totter out of the room—Yakov followed.

"I'll make my way to him… work them debts off… I swear," Yakov said, cutting off Karl's path, and putting his hand in his uncle's chest. Karl, staggering drunk, looked down at the hand and then into Yakov's face with something approaching inebriated amazement, as if some joke lay afoot.

"Right… right,… listen, would ye toil under Adelman?" Karl roared, taking the focus back to himself and leaning into Yakov's hand. "I'm the one runnin' this place… Hans declared it so. He said, 'Karl, I make thee the keeper.' Swear it on me cup! Says I. I'll manage all, ye'll see, I'll…" pausing. Karl belched again and looked glassy-eyed at

Yakov. "What did he hand over to thee?" He said, passing wind, spittle coming from his smiling, slanted mouth simultaneously as he spoke. Yakov pulled back from his uncle, the stench drifting around the room, droplets of saliva wetting his face and clothes.

Yakov waited with determination for the tirade to pass…always a tirade to get his way. Just moments ago, Karl wanted to sell off Anna if worse came to worst. Even now, he wanted Yakov to go work his debts off— nonetheless, Yakov knew the man would throw a tantrum over nothing. Already, Karl peered at Yakov from the corner of his glassy, red-rimmed eye.

Drawing himself to his full height, Yakov confronted his uncle nose to nose. "Yes, but you don't. You have done nothing to help us but drink away any income we have generated." Anna sat amazed at the strength which suddenly became apparent in her brother's stature. *Mayhaps uncoverin' the man within him lay not so distant.* She thought.

"Yer doin' this just to vex me. Out o'spite!" spat back his uncle. After all, I did fer ya! But aye, do as ye please. Off with ye then! Have me blessin'. Bah, off tomorrow if ye wish, its all the same to me!" Karl plopped heavily down into a chair near the table.

Waving his hand dismissively, Karl stood and stumbled away, lying at his favorite place by the wall, snoring instantly. Yakov stood there looking at him coolly. He seemed like a hibernating bear when he slept. Dried blood from his beating at the hands of the two goons, dried in his tangled beard, in turn wetted by the stout beer he exclusively lived on.

Was he a sicked man? Mayhaps he was, and mayhaps he was not, Yakov reminded himself. The question of morality did not stay for long in young Yakov's mind. Like a stampeding horse, concern wafted over him. His impending future, was now finally upon him.

"I caught most of that," a voice chimed in. It was Anna. She gave him a measured, worried look. "So, art thou set to follow through?

"I will."

"'Tis good then." She said, though she wanted to stop him – the moment passed. "Come, let me comb your hair."

"I don't-"

"Hush," she said, and he complied. Soon, he sat on a stool outside, looking into the horizon as Anna sat behind him. His hood fallen back. He watched Dieter wander around the field as Anna began to comb through his matted, dark hair.

Then he felt tears rise, and he knew his time as a youth lay silently in the past—just distant memories.

Chapter IV: Journey's Start

"Look at His word. The path from Jerusalem to Jericho was fraught with peril, but the journey between the two was necessary. If there was no journey, there would be no parable… and then where would we be?"

-Unknown Monk, circa 1383

The next month, the two hired hands returned, fully expecting to accost Karl once again, surprised instead to find Yakov waiting for them outside the farmhouse, dressed in his best, and only, heavy wools, a floppy hat and a blanket draped over his shoulders gave him the most protection from the weather. A drizzly rain fell in a mist and fog around them all.

This time of year, always brings the fog, Yakov reflected as he pulled the woolen blanket closer around his neck.

The guards, more dressed for the weather, wore padded caps topped with leather skullcaps; these, aside from their worn woolen gloves and an oiled cape, gave them escape from the creeping winter.

"How are you, little calf?" said one with condescension, his smile a smirk. "Where's the drunkard uncle of yours?"

"Inside, but you won't need him," Yakov said seriously, looking up to the rider, water dripping from his woolen hat. "We've decided. I'll go to Adelman and work off our farm's debt."

Peering sidewise at Yakov through the fog, the men exchanged a look and glanced back to him.

"How old are you? Ten summers? Twelve?"

"Almost fourteen," Yakov said, standing firm, with a look of determination. "And I can work for free, as far as he's concerned—all I'm working for be to pay our debt."

Yakov's wisdom could not see the danger standing as a ghostly apparition of his future behind the two guards. His youthful age would not allow him to see his fate at hand. Entering forced bondage would not provide an answer for Yakov whose mother once faced the same trap but escaped the tendrils of that slavery. Yakov, feeling a need for sacrifice, did not realize going with these men would not shield the farm from any other dire circumstances. These thoughts of a mature man never crossed his mind. The certainty of the step he chose to take felt right…in his mind…*the only step to take.*

As Yakov watched, water now pooling around his feet, the men conferred for a moment. From inside the house, Anna emerged holding a blanket over her head with one hand, a parcel of dried meats and tough bread for Yakov's journey in the other. Dieter followed at a distance, looking at them with uncertain eyes.

Anna glanced back as she covered the short distance to Yakov and the men. "Dieter, get back in the house." She called.

Turning back to the assembly outside the house, Anna said. "Karl's still sleeps? The decision's made." Anna averted her eyes, then looked at Yakov. He managed a slight smile. Again, looking to the two men on horseback, she informed them, "It be noon when he awakens."

"Have ye said goodbye to mother?" Anna asked Yakov. Noticing her brother's grimace, she quickly changed the focus of the conversation. Karl's abuse of alcohol never did bode well with Yakov. The decision for Yakov to leave with the men could only be blamed on Karl and his inability to follow his brother Hans' request to care for the homestead and the family. To Anna's frustration, Yakov now became an instrument of a patriarchal society, to lead by example, something Anna thought should have been her responsibility.

Yakov nodded quietly, keeping his face carefully blank. In truth, his last meeting with his mother played out like every other meeting between them over the past few years—silent and painful.

From the entryway, Yakov saw Olga sitting up, staring at the far wall. She held a bowl of porridge on her lap. He carefully sat down beside her and, taking the small bowl from her, he began to feed her, sliding a wooden spoon with the morning porridge into her mouth. Placing a hand gently on her forehead, he held her head back so she could swallow. No indication of recognition, no light of humanity, shown in her eyes.

Outside once more and seeing Yakov shaken by their mother's reactions to him, Anna felt Yakov's depression.

Quickly, she disappeared into the house to reappear, holding yet another half-loaf of bread. Ignoring his protests, Anna packed the bread in with the rest of his belongings with quiet intensity.

"Boy!" one of the tax collectors called. "We agreed. Come with us—we leave today. Two more farmstead visits lay ahead and thence back to Helmstedt. Get your belongings and do't quickly."

The fog began to rise slightly. At least, Yakov thought with a sigh, *this would make travel a bit more pleasant.* However, he also knew the sop of wet woolens would continue with him for a while as they dried in the rays of what little the sun might provide.

"Aye, I have what I need," Yakov said, calmly listing to himself *one change of clothes, a few ha'pennies, the dried meat and bread, a wooden crucifix carved by Anna, all now wrapped in an extra woolen blanket.*

"Be he safe w'ye?" Anna asked the men, her protective blanket now soaked with water.

One of them hawked spittle into the mud on the other side of his horse, and peering back, he gave her a dead-eyed look. "Nay, one's nay safe in these times, young lady. Worry for yerself, as me mother wont t'say."

Eager not to cause a problem for Yakov, Anna ventured uncertainly. "Aye, a wise woman."

The man barked with bitter laughter. "Aye. she twas tha'. She died all the same. Come on, boy!" He chortled to Yakov.

Yakov hugged Anna and Dieter one last time before walking through the gathering mud to the men. *They seemed bigger now, more like forlorn heroes in some forgotten story; yet, just hired thugs,* Yakov thought, being pulled onto a sway-backed mare ridden by one of the men.

Riding off, Yakov chanced a look back. The farmhouse receded behind him. Anna stood in the road, water and mud around her feet, her hair dripping. Both she and Dieter stood in the doorway waving their goodbye. The giant elm tree sheltering the house as if to ward off the wetness of the day and forbidding times ahead stood strong against rising mist and fog. *When would he lay eyes on the elm or see his kin again,* he wondered.

***

The first day passed into the next. The mist and fog dissipated each day by midday, but a chill still entered the bones of the small company. Over time, Yakov learned to tell the two men apart as Ingmar and Jon. Jon, with his dirty blond hair and wearing a dark gambeson, stood taller than the bearded, unruly Ingmar.

Leaving home three days before, the small band camped beneath a cloudless sky. The mud of the past days, now dried and firm, made passage easier. A full moon provided an eerie brilliance to the night, where any stars to be seen lost their pinpoint appearance to the brightness of the moon. Sentinel-like shadows of tall trees rose around Yakov and his fellow travelers. Only the occasional sound of an owl in the forest or a wolf in the distance broke the silence of the night. Ingmar limped around fixing a fire to warm the trio and ward off animals. Yakov lay on his blanket nearby, his head against a log looking up at those pinpoints of light, the few stars he could see through the moonlight. His stomach felt sick. He missed home.

On the fourth day, the trio road out of the forest. The trees stood as silent statues, losing their leaves patiently waiting the long sleep of winter. Winding along the dried mire of previous days, they arrived at a homestead intending to collect taxes or rents as planned. The farmhouse stood on a hill. The fields, yellow all around, appeared in a similar unkempt state as Karl's keeping of the Symon fields. The thatched roof of the two-room home seemed ready to cave in. Daub loosened from the outside walls fell to the ground, in places leaving brown patches of wattle, wooden slats, exposed. As Ingmar, Jon, and Yakov approached on horseback, a weedy man with scraggly hair walked out into the road and stood a few feet away from a tree stump used as a hitching post which jutted from the ground. Jon dismounted. Looping his reigns around the stump, he walked toward the man. From a distance, Yakov could see a small pouch pass between the two. Ingmar, with Yakov sitting behind him, waited patiently as Jon returned, satisfied with the exchange.

"At least one soul settled his dues," Jon said with a wry tone to his voice. "Mayhaps old man Adelman shan't be as vexed."

Ingmar grunted a response as the riders moved on. Two more days of traveling awaited them. The horses' ambling gate brought on the drowsiness as before. Each time they set camp, the men made sparse conversation by the fire, content to ignore Yakov. For his part, Yakov would wander around to stretch his legs or lie on his back on the grass with nostalgic eyes.

Creating a good bed for the night became his only constant duty. The early winter dampness began to take its toll on good rest, but Yakov learned to make do. Wriggling to move or extract a small stone or fallen branch from under his blanket, he lay back to reminisce. Gone from him now, the comfort of Anna and Dieter felt so far away. The sounds of Anna's bossy voice or Dieter's quiet smiles unfolded around him. He missed these most. He even missed the everyday chores and the lukewarm porridge in the morning. Yakov chuckled. Then, following a deep, longing sigh, he slept.

Emerging from the woods on the dry road, Jon, Ingmar, and Yakov found themselves at yet another farm, a much larger holding. The fields and home were in better repair than they had encountered a couple of days back. Near a gate to the front of the mud and waddle home, a rotund woman who called herself Grunhilda met the group. She and her sons managed the land here. This time, Yakov dismounted and hung back, holding the horses as they grazed on the yellow grass along the edge of the road. The horses, calmly resigned to the break in travel, munched the grass with an occasional glance at any surrounding noise. Jon dismounted. Following his partner's lead, Ingmar dismounted also. Jon warily walked toward the farmhouse, this time with Ingmar in tow.

As they approached the hitching post where Grunhilda stood, she retreated inside the house. Soon, a young man, sandy-haired and stout of build, opened the door and began to talk with Jon. The encounter soon turned into shouts and waiving of arms by the man. Suddenly, everything happened so quickly that Yakov found it troublesome to understand the cause. Without hesitation, Ingmar kicked the burly man in the crotch and pulled him squealing from the house. Throwing the injured man to the ground, Ingmar continued to kick him about the head and stomach.

A man, younger than the first, suddenly darted out the door with wide eyes and a snarl, only to get a cudgel alongside of his head from Jon. The lad abruptly found himself, feet in the air and parallel to the ground from the force of Jon's blow. He dropped hard to the ground where he lay unmoving. Jon put his cudgel into his belt and calmly walked into the farmhouse, he remained for what seemed to Yakov a long time. No noise came from within. Outside, Ingmar sat with his knee on the first son's wheezing chest. Yakov continued to watch with curiosity and wide eyes the casual violence. Soon, Jon walked out brandishing a small leather pouch, whereupon both he and Ingmar returned to the grazing horses and Yakov, breathing easily.

"Old woman give ye trouble?" Ingmar asked, spitting.

"A resilient old bird," Jon chuckled. "She did brandish a blade in me direction, but in the end, she parted with her coin. Not the full sum, mind you, but just a taste, just enough to suffice." He said, holding up the pouch.

"Mayhaps this time he'll toss a bit extra for our troubles." Ingmar barked with laughter.

"Who, Adelman?" Jon joined in the laughter. "He'd sooner wed us to his daughters than pay us a penny more."

Yakov listened awe-struck by the exchange of words with some concern. Looking at Yakov, Ingmar could not contain his amusement at Yakov's expense and roared with laughter. "You're putt'n a fright in the poor lad, Jon." Reassuring he continued. "Fear not, youngster! Adelman doth settle his debts—he may not be a saint, but he's no fouler than any other soul in these days."

"And ye won't be workin' fer money in any case," Jon added. "Yer only workin' the debt off. He'll be good to ye—he will." He said, looking at Ingmar with a wink of his eye.

Assured, taking their word for it with some skepticism, Yakov stayed silent. He felt nostalgic for a simpler time, inevitably anxious about his future. He wondered if there could be anything he could do if things really did end up less than good—what could he do? Yakov felt a profound sense of helpless loneliness well up inside him, threatening to spill over as he watched the clouds pass above them.

Spurring the horses on, the repetitive gate brought on a dreamy haze as these uncommon three continued down the road. Yakov noted the fields on either side of the road were turning slowly into the greys of winter. The late fall colors lacked the emerald, green color of summer. Instead, a certain grayish-yellow clung to the roots of the grass. Yakov watched it blur past through drooping eyes and the calming effect of the smells of the forest filling his nostrils. The late day sun, now low in the sky, promised a short ride before setting camp.

Later that night, as they sat around the campfire, Yakov lay awake on a wool blanket, dressed in his woolen clothes and a second blanket wrapped around his shoulders and waist. The night was dark. The full moon of the earlier part of the journey was now gone, leaving only the darkest of nights. Even the light of the fire appeared to struggle against the black of the forest shadow. Yakov, alert to night sounds, occasionally heard the brush shuffle or a branch crack beyond that cone of firelight. Looking up beyond the tops of the silhouettes of trees against the sky, he now could see the innumerable pinpoints of light in the night sky. So many points of light hung in the sky, their appearance created a cloud-like veil to the dark of the unknown.

Yakov sat in an uneasy silence with Ingmar, who propped himself awake against a log a short distance away, keeping watch as Jon snored the first half of the night away. He sat polishing his cudgel with a dirty rag and spittle. Eventually, putting it aside, he drew a small dagger from his boot and began to sharpen it with a flat stone, coarse and mottled with shining flecks. He caught Yakov's glance.

"D'ye know where I got this?" he asked without preamble, the firelight reflecting off the blade.

Yakov shook his head hesitantly. Ingmar gave him a bitter smile.

"Me father killed hisself with it," Ingmar said conversationally as he continued to sharpen it. Yakov took in a slow, audible breath.

"The village gave him a woodland grave for that sin, far from the holy church's embrace. The dagger passed into me mum's hands, and upon her passin', it found its way t'me." Ingemar explained.

He gave Yakov a piercing look. 'But I ponder, what will become of it when I shuffle off this mortal coil? This blade's tale commenced with me sire, yet where shall its journey conclude?" Ingemar mused.

Yakov looked at him quietly, wondering, not knowing what to say. Finally, he turned away, disturbed. Above him, the night sky glittered with stars. An owl's hoot, a flurried flapping of wings, and a squeal could be heard as the large bird plucked a rabbit from the glade beyond the circle of firelight. Insects hummed quietly in the dark behind Yakov; the fire continued to crackle as Ingmar continued to sharpen his dagger mechanically.

As he drifted to sleep, Yakov wondered briefly where the coming days would take him—but wherever his path eventually led, certainty took its cue.

A journey now lay ahead of him. A journey lost to any wisdom of a young man of fourteen.

Chapter V: Apples

"This year, the church orchards are ripe with apples, red, green, gold, but they are not the best of apples. The best of apples and the best of men are to be found on the road to Helmstedt..."

-Unknown Monk, circa 1385

A new morning and a stiff breeze welcomed the heat of a boiling broth steeping over a small campfire. Yakov relented to add some dried strips of meat packed for him by Anna a week ago. Initially garlic gave the strongest flavor; however, Jon foraged enough to find a few wild herbs to add to the broth and balance the taste. Finally, Yakov spooned a bowl of the hot savory liquid to Jon and Ingmar, who eagerly sipped in the warmth, braving the chilly wind.

"We should be reaching Helmstedt in a few days," Jon announced, looking at Yakov. "Listen, boy—are ye certain about this?"

"Why would I not be?" Yakov answered cautiously.

"Yer squanderin' precious years of thy life an' fer wha'? Four walls and a roof what drips when it rains?"

"I be doin' it fer me family," Yakov said hotly, before remembering himself. "'Tis me place bein' the eldest son."

"Leave the runt alone, Jon," Ingmar grunted with finality. The small band finished their food quietly. Soon, packed and mounted, the trio road on once more.

The three travelled for the better part of the day in silence. Once or twice one of the men would begin to sing in a tuneless voice. The sound of their voices would trail away on the silent road either forgetting the song or just the monotony of the journey. Then the silence would return for a time. The country grew woodsier now. The trees hunched over the road, intertangling branches in a broad arch, occasionally appearing like old men, or standing in proud, regal regiments far into the distance. The grass, more sparce now as well from lack of sunlight, still appeared mildly sick.

Circling down a hill, the trio found themselves entering a copse of trees. The horses slowed to a shallow step, neighing nervously. Ingmar and Jon exchanged a quarried glance. From behind Ingmar, Yakov leaned out to see what lay ahead. Not too far away, under a tree with knotted red bark, lay a dying horse. It neighed pitifully as they neared, one of its hooves kicking weakly at the dirt. Their own horses began sidestepping nervously.

Jon dismounted. "Poor Girl," he said quieting the injured horse.

Ingmar paused briefly, dismounted, took the reins of Jon's horse from Jon's proffered hand and steadied the two horses. Yakov did not move. "Easy," he said quietly, stroking his horse's muzzle and working to keep the two horses calm.

"Look here," Jon said "See--leg's not right."

"Easy girl, easy." Jon repeated, petting the neck of the horse. "'Tis bent all wrong. I think it be broken," he said to Jon.

"Where be her rider?" Yakov asked, from his perch, looking over the neck of his mount.

Glancing a look at Yakov and then the mare, Jon, and Ingmar, realized the saddled and fully tacked horse bore no rider. Puzzled, they looked around, but the trio found no body or injured person anywhere. No campfire smoked nearby.

"Either he be dead or he be a heartless bastard," Ingmar said angrily. "Ye don't leave a creature t'suffer."

Ingmar handed Jon the reins of their horses and drawing his knife from its scabbard, he moved towards the suffering horse. Startled by the move, Yakov looked on not fully realizing Ingmar's intent. Death of any creature was not new to Yakov, but he instinctively croaked out a weak "Nay, Ingmar, Stop," as he understood what would happen next.

"It be nay our problem, Ingmar," Jon growled to his partner. Ingmar hushed the struggling animal, as he drew close. Gently patting the injured horse's neck, he placed his knife under the horses' throat, and with one fluid stroke, slit her neck. He patted her again, a tear running down his cheek. Blood ran freely out of the wound, between the fingers of his hand, pumping with the horse's last awareness in this world. The mare's wide eyes, confused, as life trickled away.

Ingmar whispered, "'Tis okay me beauty. Rest now. Shhhhh…" The horse's quivering hooves stilled and with a final, shuddering breath, she lay quiet, eyes glossing over. Ingmar wiped the bloody dagger on the horse's neck. Then with a sigh, standing he slid the knife back into its scabbard, and grimly returned to his horse wiping his hands on his pants. He stood for a few moments cradling his own horse's head, calming her nervousness. Yakov, somewhat amazed, realized Ingmar and Jon could be understanding too.

The small band began to move again. Yakov looked down at the milky, unseeing gaze of the dead horse and forced himself to turn away. Thinking about those lesson on the farm, the scene just completed continued to disturb him.

He still remembered the death of their goat, old Greta. An infected wound putrefied despite Anna's poultices. Greta, then put down, cost the family a good portion of food in a time of need. In the end, the family simply buried it; however, in the fall, when the crop started to fail, Karl placed the blame on the goat's corpse and the infection.

Yakov remembered, an entire year after burying the animal, Karl forced Yakov to dig up the desecrated corpse and burn it. The state of corruption of the creature sat on Yakov's mind, which both horrified and fascinated Yakov. He felt the same unknowable dread looking over the horse freshly slain by Ingmar.

Quickly and quietly on their way again, Yakov settled on the hips of the horse and up behind Ingmar. Without warning Ingmar, leading, slowed the small group and pointed. "What's that ahead?" he muttered. Near the trees, a shape moved in the shadows.

Ingmar, Jon, and Yakov edged their horses cautiously closer to the woods ahead and toward the last appearance of the shape. The shape seemed to disappear behind a large tree a few feet beyond the road. Approaching, the trio found a large knobby apple tree. Some of the fruit still on its branches and some fallen to the ground, rotting where it lay.

"Who be there!" called Jon, dismounting, and drawing his cudgel, as he and Ingmar slowly inched closer to the tree.

"Let 'em be, whoever they be." Yakov found himself saying weakly, hoping to avoid more violence, but the two did not seem to hear him.

"Come out and we won't hurt ye," Jon continued in a reasonable voice.

"Go away!" came a frightened, high-pitched boy's voice from the shadows behind the tree.

Jon and Ingmar paused and exchanged glances. In less than a minute a youth, a little younger than Yakov, appeared from behind the tree, trying to avoid the two men. Now crouching on opposite sides of the tree, Ingmar quickly grasped the boy around the waist, and Jon, moving just as fast, grabbed the young boy's feet. Together they carried the young person to the road, where the two men set him down forcing him to stay still.

"Wha' be ye doin' here, boy?" Jon asked, looking as sternly as possible at the shivering child in front of the trio.

The boy, much thinner than Yakov, with brown curls which fell down his shoulders, and cropped short in front just above his wide eyes, gave him the appearance of a child running away. Starving, thirsty, and frightened with delicate cheeks and sunken eyes presented a gaunt face. Sweat and blood stained his patchy tunic, and from head-to-toe, dust rose in a cloud of obvious neglect.

"What's that matter t'thee?" the boy asked rudely, then eyeing Jon's cudgel he took a step back.

Jon's eyebrows rose a bit at the child's boldness while tapping the cudgel in his open hand. Shocked by the affront from a mere boy, Jon reacted, "Well, we've a strong 'un here." Seeing the boy cower a bit he hung the cudgel tucking it in over his belt and with an amused expression, gestured to Ingmar to do the same.

The youth, glancing around, now seeing Yakov for the first time, looked at him with confused suspicion. "Who be he?" He quavered.

"Boy's travelling wi' us t'find work—but enough about us," Jon gruffed with an easy smile. "Yer name?"

"Mikkel." He said, now shivering in the coolness of the late afternoon autumn air.

"We laid eyes on a mare further down the way there." Jon pointed. "Yer horse I reckon?"

"She be… well, aye… mine." He said with worried expression. "She be a good girl, she is. I think she broke her leg. I've picked apples fer her, see, but her leg be…"

Mikkel paused as Jon wistfully nodded his head. He looked at Ingmar's deadpan face, then at Yakov's guilty eyes. Realization came to Mikkel, his eyes widening with awareness. "Ye killed her, didn't ye?" he asked quietly. Looking down at the apples fallen at his feet, tears began to well in his eyes. With deep sobs he said, "I don't blame... I mean, I knew I should have. I just ..."

"Where'd ye find a mare like that?" Ingmar asked, grabbing the boy's jersey, a forceful, gravely tone to his voice, and staring into the Mikkel's eyes. Seeing Mikkel's freight, Ingmar released the boy. Turning back to his companions, "She'd all the traits of a good horse, beautiful, even though her ribs showed. Yer mare obviously weren't fed for a time." To Mikkel again he asked suspiciously, "Where'd ye get your grubby little mitts on her, boy? These clothes and yer grime places ye nothing more than a stable hand."

"Ingmar!" Jon said warningly, shooting him a look.

"Nay, it be fair," Mikkel said dejectedly, shivering a bit harder. He slumped against a nearby tree. "I was runnin' cause of problems, ya see? I took her a day or two back, up north from some bandit fella. He was doin' his business, and me, after them bad folks came to my village and took everything, I had nothin', honest! So, umm...I kinda..."

Rolling his eyes and turning towards Jon and Yakov, Ingmar chuckled, then headed toward the bush just off the road. Over his shoulder, as he untied the front of his breeches, he chided Mikkel, "Thou art a spry orphan who stole a horse and rode her till her leg gave way." Ingmar unbelieving, said flatly, winking at Jon, "I be goin' to take a piss. See this little squirrel doesn't steal me horse." Jon could not hold his poise any longer and roared with laughter, spittle spewing out of his mouth. Yakov, nearly covered with the spray, stepped away quickly.

Ignoring Jon's amusement, Ingmar stepped up to the bushes to relieve himself. Mikkel, embarrassed, looked away, muttering in a small voice, as the others continued to watch, "What else was I s'posed to do, huh? What else? Runnin' or starvin', that's all I saw. I guess I coulda slaughtered her for food, but why bother. So I just ran…why did I run, you ask? There was nowhere else to go, I guess that's why." Wetness filling his eyes again, he continued with a sigh, "Why did I run?"

"Who be ye anyway lad?" Jon gruffly retorted, exasperated, setting his mirth aside.

"I be just a boy mindin' my own business tryin' to get as far away from trouble and harm as I can." Mikkel retorted, then withdrawing, a bit frightened by Jon. "Mum, she be a seamstress, and me da, he a tinker for a tiny hanse town just a few days' ride from here. Bandits come, mercenaries maybe, so I guess, and attacked us a second time. From their chatter I gathered they looked fer food and plunder. We'd none to give. Them scoundrels set our shack ablaze with me mum and da inside. They just killed 'em," Mikkel said trying to hold down sobs. "I escaped because my morning chore was to gather water the town well. Hearing a clammer coming from the direction of my home, I simply ran into the woods and hid. While hiding one of the bandits came by. He dismounted to take care of his business.

While he squatted over a log, I stole his horse. Ok," he pleaded. "I am just a boy."

"Okay, relax lad," Jon said, walking over to Mikkel, and then looking over at Yakov once more. His mission to find boys for Adelman grew in his mind as he remembered. "Ye could come with us."

"Where?" Startled, Mikkel said in confusion, "Why?"

"Yakov, give the boy one of yer blankets. You have two." Jon commanded.

"We can find ye work—decent work, as good as any man can hope fer in these times," Jon smiled encouragingly. "See the lad there? That be young Yakov, going that-a-ways right this instant to pay his family debts."

Yakov nudged his horse towards Mikkel holding out a blanket, happy to have the new companion, "Here," he said. "Take this."

Mikkel, now shaking from the cold, looked at Yakov, dully feeling the possibility of a trap. Yakov dismounted with the blanket. He hesitantly walked over to Mikkel and gave him a typical farmer's greeting—head slightly bowed, hand on his heart. Mikkel returned the greeting clumsily, before looking back at Jon for assurance.

Yakov again held out the blanket, which Mikkel wrapped around his shoulders.

"We be headed fer Helmstedt," Jon said. "And ye, well, y'don't have much t'do here, do ye? There, ye'd be working for a decent man…, about as decent as a merchant be likely to get anyways. Y'll have food, shelter, and wages, however little."

Mikkel looked at Jon, then at Yakov, then down at the dirt near his feet. Rubbing the tears from his eyes he offered, "We should take some of these apples with us," accepting the adventure ahead.

"So, yer comin'?" Jon asked.

"Aye."

Jon beamed knowing Adleman would be pleased. Yakov, unaware of Jon's intent, gave Mikkel an encouraging smile. At that instant, Ingmar returned with a dour expression.

"What's happenin'?" Ingmar asked with annoyance wanting to know what had transpired. Jon just gave him a satisfied look.

"Yakov's to be sittin' with ye."

"Why, Jon? Don't like brats?"

"Mikkel's comin' with us," said Jon, walking over to his horse. "An' yer either ridin' with Yakov or him," he said pointing back to Mikkel.

Ingmar gave Yakov a long-suffering look rolling his eyes. "Get on the horse, runt."

"Okay Mikkel," Jon said, reaching for Mikkel's hand, "up ya'come." Still shivering from the cold, the warmth against Jon's back and sitting on the horse did not go unnoticed as Mikkel positioned himself.

***

In camp that night Yakov propped himself against a stout maple tree a short way from the fire—significantly less bothered by Ingmar and Jon's attention with Mikkel to take some of the jibbing. Again, the night, dark, showed only a sliver of moon. Jon kept first watch. Mikkel lay awake not far from Yakov, looking up into the inky black of the night. He watched as the moon ambled across the sky above. "How long?" he muttered to himself. *Until morning...until he could find home again.* Lost, in his thoughts, he knew he would never know.

Pinpoints of starlight flickered on and off as Mikkel tried to make something familiar out of nothing. He and Yakov spoke little at first, but Yakov, gradually, felt a growing curiosity toward Mikkel. Boys his own age never spent much time with him because work on the farm always needed to be finished first. The months of festival, spring and fall, brought families together from all the neighboring farmsteads, an opportunity for boys and girls his age to make or renew acquaintances and for sharing.

Still wondering how to start a conversation, Jon sitting nearby spoke to Mikkel, breaking the silence between the two boys.

"What be yer village name, boy?" Jon asked.

"Ye would nay have heard of it. Wolutenburg."

"Yer right, never heard of it," replied Jon trying to continue the conversation.

"'Twas nay special, but it be wonderful," Mikkel said wistfully, looking into the firelight and pulling his blanket close around his shoulders. The chill of the day remained, but the warmth of the fire and the blanket given him by Yakov now staved off the cold.

"The fields be green as can be, and the old men and the women would tell stories every night," Mikkel continued. Food was nay plentiful, but there be enough, just enough. My father be a barrel-maker, a cooper, as well as a tinker. I guess I would have been too." *Mikkel the cooper's son…Mikkel Cooperson, or maybe Tinkerson* he mused.

Divorcing from the stupor of the moment, Mikkel looked at Yakov with misty eyes. Yakov, returning the gaze, wondered how Mikkel felt, *nothing to go back to, nothing to anchor to. After all,* Yakov mused, *the Symon farmstead gave him a place to call home…not Mikkel though.*

Time passed. Eventually the conversation picked up again. "A craftsman or a farmer I would be then." Yakov said suddenly, breaking the quiet.

"A craftsman?" Jon asked, entering the conversation once again, amused. "I didn't know Karl knew anything but drink."

"Nay him, Karl's my uncle, my father's brother," Yakov said painfully thinking of the beatings he used to receive from Karl. "Me father, Hans be his proper name, Johan Hans Symon." Pausing for a momentary thought,

Yakov continued, "I don't remember much of the last four or five years or all of what he used to do, but I know he used to sell his carvings in Helmstedt. From days long past, I remember him sitting out in the sun, on the steps of our home, carving small wooden shapes with a smile. He created little boxes and statues or pins and needles of wood, or he worked our fields following oxen and the plow. He could work an ox to pull our plow, encouraging the straightest furrows." Yakov mused, then continued, "The rest, being gone at times fer long periods from home, he never talked much about, and then one day he did nay return."

He paused for a while, "It be hard fer me to remember how he looked." Yakov stared into the dancing light of the fire, tears now welling in the corners of his eyes, yearning for his father and his gentle kindness.

"Did he die?" Mikkel asked, looking at Yakov.

Yakov shook his head, pulling the wools closer around him. "Nay, he… left," he replied quietly. Where he went, I don't know, neither did Anna or Dieter, or my uncle. Sickness kept me mother down for a long time before his leavin'. She became difficult to help. I think…sometimes she…" he paused. "In the night, sometimes, my sister and I could hear them talkin'. I think we knew father'd leave… Anna would know more, but things worsened after he left, Mother hinted occasionally…things may not always have been as they seemed."

"From my village," said Mikkel soberly, "we knew about the mercenaries—we even used to give them tribute before each winter to leave us alone. Then one day, our village headsman, Little-Father Grimmer, went to petition the local lord of our manor. Gone seven days and seven nights, we waited. He finally returned with empty hands. Somehow, the lowlifes heard we appealed for help. They attacked us in our small village. Their anger focused on Little-Father Grimmer who they caught visiting his daughter. They dragged him behind his own horse until all the breath be gone from him… his terrible screamin' stopped."

"Should nay have appealed to the nobility," Jon chimed in, overhearing the discussion. "The men of the garland and crown don't care for we humble lot, not a whit. They be nay the knights of myths and tales."

"Ne're one came," Mikkel muttered, barely coherent. "At first, just me, mother, father, the smith, and his wife huddled together near the forge. We left at night moving into the woods to hide until we could return to our small home.

Mikkel, anger in his voice, continued. "Not long after that, them scoundrels, they come back for plundrin again, and they caught us, just a few of us, tryin' to lay our folks to rest from their first foray… In all the chaos… and fightin'… our cottage, it burned down to nothin'… The rest, well, I told that part before… I be the only one," Mikkel finished in resignation, "… to escape."

Silence lay over the band of four as firelight accented the concern on each face. Jon reached into his bag, drew out four apples, and threw each boy and Ingmar one collected from the tree up the road. Yakov caught his, looked at it and nodding to Jon, took a bite. Looking around at each of the small company, he could see thoughts reflected in the countenance of his newfound friends...or maybe adversaries; he did not know. As he bit into the sweet, slightly bitter apple, the taste felt good to Yakov's throat as the juice trickled soothingly down.

***

After two more days of alternating between riding and walking, Mikkel seemed to grow brighter. A more even eating schedule worked wonders. The activity put some color in his cheeks, and though still gaunt, he appeared livelier. Wary of Ingmar's temper, however, Mikkel spent most of his time on foot with Yakov, trailing behind the older men. With laughter and some seriousness always in the telling, Yakov and Mikkel exchanged numerous stories. Not much could be found common between the two, but they soon became fast friends.

Yakov told Mikkel more about his own family, and Mikkel gradually revealed deeper stories about the village from which he came. Too, skirting around numerous topics which each assumed the other would just as soon avoid, became subjects remaining secure in the mind of each, behind their eyes and staring into the distance, could reminisce.

The wind, no more than a breeze, bit into the four as they traveled announcing the morning of the third day. They could see a hint of smoke above the trees not far ahead. Stopping to take a gulp from his water-skin, Jon nudged his horse towards what appeared to be a village a mile or two away. He turned to look back at the two boys, assuring himself they were alert to what lay ahead.

"We be near Helmstedt now. Mayhaps we can reach there today." He said with a smile.

Hearing that news, Yakov gave a sigh of relief. Though saddle-sores seemed to grow on saddle sores and ploughing a field for days on end could not compare with how his back felt from all the riding, the foursome's arrival should be soon.

Wind, first gentle, turned relentlessly to whistling fury. The intensity of the wind brought on an ever-growing foreboding of winter. Colored leaves laying at the base of trees, turned into whirlwind slaps, which stung any uncovered part of the face and signaled worse weather to come.

Now reigning towards Helmstedt, the four became a curious sight to other travelers passing them by. The two boys, wrapped in their blankets, now huddled against the backs of Ingmar and Jon , and partially protected from the wind, wondered what fate would be waiting.

Chapter VI: Good Folk

"The nobles have their great leaders, but among the commoners are good folk... and the Good Samaritan in the parable was among the latter, not the former."

-Unknown Monk, circa 1384

Anna, leaning against the doorpost outside the entrance of the farmhouse, looked across the now-harvested fields of stubble. She stood quietly with a basket in her hand, remembering the warmth of summer past, seeing now the grey clouds forming overhead. The fall breeze blew stray strands of her hair across her face.

She looked with uncertainty to the horizon for a fleeting moment, then turned to the old tree and walked slowly towards a small, fenced family plot. The big elm, planted by her grandfather, now a symbol of family, stood to the east of the farmhouse just on the other side of the road and at the edge of the now-harvested fields. Beneath the spreading tree, in a freshly fenced-off portion, lay a fresh grave with a stack of stones for a headstone. From her basket, Anna drew a few fall wildflowers picked from a nearby thicket and looked at the grave with curiosity.

Their mother, Olga, died only a few days after Yakov left. From some far-off thought, Anna wondered, *did Mother love Yakov more?* Tears streamed from her eyes, and guilt swelled within her. *If the only reason Mother remained alive was out of love for him… if that were the case, did she not love Dieter or me? Didn't I keep the farm going for the past few years, pushing Yakov and Dieter through daily chores while taking care of her? Wasn't I equal to any man on the homestead?*

Anna found her mother hunched forward in her bed when she took breakfast to her in the morning only a day earlier. Today, staring at the lonely grave, she thought of Yakov, and how mother spent her days encouraging him to go find work as befitting an elder son. *Our uncle Karl refused to accept the family responsibility given him by her father,* she remembered. *All be left to Anna to provide. Mother still looked to Karl more. I did all I could with Dieter in tow and payments or taxes coming due soon,* she struggled with the thought. *Could Mother not stand to let her young Yakov go? Yet it happened that way with Yakov gone to find work. Olga now dead, left the care of the farm to me with little Dieter to raise…until Yakov could return.*

Anna clenched her hands at her sides, growling through unwanted tears. *If only I had been born a son,* Anna thought to herself bitterly. *Everything could have been avoided. Karl would never have taken charge, nor Yakov encouraged to leave.* Tears streaming down her face, she placed the flowers as tenderly as she could on the grave … as though placing them in her mother's lap. "Mama, please, I need your help," she sobbed, kneeling down.

"Oh, but I did love you, mother," Anna blurted, after a pause, confused. She stood and turned away from the grave wiping her wet face with the hem of her dress. A deep anger growled from her throat. She was often too busy caring for everything else to spend much time with her mother. Anything she said now seemed hollow. Turning back her anger subsiding, "Be at peace, mama," Anna canted softly. "Be at peace."

From her contrition, she slowly turned and gathered up her skirt and basket. Glancing in the direction of the house and then down at the path, she headed back to the house. It only took a moment to cover the distance to the house to check on the evening's stew. Almost immediately, Anna became aware of movement coming along the road. Several caravans, pulled by sturdy mules, rounded the bend in the lane a quarter mile away and headed in the direction of the farmhouse.

Anna stopped abruptly and looked on with undisguised suspicion. At the front moved a relatively ramshackle caravan drawn by two mules, a stained tarp pulled over a rib-arched back. In the driver's seat, a hunched figure held the reigns. He wore a black hat at a jaunty angle. At least two more caravans followed.

"Uncle!" Anna called out, alarmed. "Uncle Karl!"

From inside the house, Anna could hear Karl stumble toward the door, rubbing sleep from his eyes despite the late hour of the morning. He began to grumble something but halted as he looked at the sight before him.

"Why that's not right at all, not right at all," he muttered, walking ahead with his chest pushed out like a festival strongman. Anna resisted the urge to roll her eyes, and rushed to check on Dieter inside the house. Reassured of his safety, Anna stopped at the cook-pot, gave the stew another quick turn and half-ran back outside. Not too far from the house, she spied her uncle standing in his dark-grey tunic, talking to a dismounted man from the caravan. Karl's chest-high posture feigned authority, his hands resting lightly on his waist.

Anna drew nearer to her uncle and the newcomer. She could see the young man was only half-listening to Karl. Karl's rummy speech and lack of balance were getting the better of him. He tried to talk. The young man, now standing up straight, blond curls sticking out from below his black hat, his faded green doublet worn over thick black leggings, gave Anna a confident smile. He clearly ignored Karl, his focus on Anna as her uncle droned on.

"… and 'tis a man's right to know why 'nother man breaches his borders, nay? That be right, borders! This land's mine…or mine to mind, and I am its caretaker… but borders and border-hoppers! That be what wars be made of, sir. 'Tis all about this...ye know. Now, would… tell me yer… name, hm? Do y'hear me? Sir!"

"Who be you?" Anna asked the man curtly as he continued to ignore Karl, who, looking simultaneously exasperated, furious, and frightened, kept on his rambling.

"Sieghart," the man replied with a winning grin. Square-jawed and dark-eyed, with deep dimples formed in his cheeks, he smiled. Something stirred deep within Anna bringing new feelings. Disoriented for a moment, she took a step back. A shiver, forming little bumps on her skin, moved over her body in a wave from her head to her toes.

"Now listen, lad, these here…" interrupted Karl.

"…Are your fields, 'tis I'm aware, good sir," Sieghart cut in, still looking at Anna, his smile a chuckle. He returned his attention to Karl and continued, "But we need only a place to spend a few days, having been on the road for several days now and are grown quite weary. Allowing a piece of yer field there to build a warm fire and cook hot food would help to restore our strength."

"We've got a stew simmerin' o'er the hearth, but there ain't near enough to feed all of you," Anna said emphatically, jumping into the conversation. Realizing her abrupt response to Sieg, she pulled her emotions in check, blushed, and turned away.

"Oh, but we have supplies, and we be more than willing to share 'em," Sieghart said, again looking quickly at Karl for his approval and then in Anna's direction with his alarming smile. "All we need is a place to set camp nearby." Returning to Karl, he continued, "We'll be stayin' here, but not more 'an a week, mind ye. We can pay for our lodgin', and we can tend to our own business, but we'd be much obliged if someone could lend a hand with cookin'. He looked back at Anna, his smiling eyes fixed on hers.

Anna groaned quietly to herself and turned away, clenching her fists, for every part of her wanted to scream. *Men!* she thought, fury raising an ugly face again in her emotional reflection. *Why must I be the servant?* Sieg immediately pulled back, his smile fading with confusion, from Anna not knowing what caused her reaction.

Karl suddenly, not wanting to lose the opportunity for his own purposes, interrupted Anna… "Ye said pay for yer stay. That be a fine sentiment," he addressed Sieg. "I respect a man who expects nothin' fer free. I do! What d'ye say for… five pennies a night?" Karl asked, his eyes gleaming as he glanced at his niece. Anna rolled her eyes and stepped away.

"And will yer fair daughter help with our meals? Sieg asked with contrition to Anna. I must confess our stews are too thin and taste of mud," Sieghart said apologetically. "But from what I smell of whate'er ye be cookin' for yerselves, I gather ye know well how to cook."

"Oh, she be not my daughter….fine girl, but nay… daughter…nope," grinning through his slurring stupor, Karl continued. "Just me niece…but fine girl," he blurted, wobbling close enough for Sieghart to catch a whiff of Karl's fowled breath. "Of course, she'll help you! …She will," Karl said, looking sternly toward where Anna now stood, holding Dieter at her side.

"Nay, I won't," Anna suddenly burst in. "Uncle, we don't even know who these people be!"

Sieghart, regaining his composure after Karl's pitch, stepped back and gave Anna a bow. Already flush from anger, her blush deepened as he straightened and addressed her again. "We might be a bit rough 'round the edges, but we be decent folk, ye see. I aim to make sure there's nothin' to grumble 'bout," he said, offering a humble bow. "I didn't mean no offense, Miss,"

Anna sputtered for a moment, then caught Karl's eye. Five pennies a night was more than fair. She could see the message clearly in Karl's eyes: *Shut yer mouth, we need this.* So, she turned and exited, her face burning with anger and embarrassment. Most of her embarrassment came at the expense of her drunken uncle. Too, as young woman, she lacked the wisdom in reading the intentions of most men, including Sieghart or her uncle Karl. This lack of experience sometimes undermined her ability to make suitable decisions for the family. Again, she felt a bit used by the older men. Behind her, she could hear Karl telling the visitors where to set up camp. Suddenly, furious again, Anna entered the thatched-roof home and began vigorously stirring the stew.

Dieter, watching most of this play out, came to sit near her and put his hand in her's, trying to make the world right for her once again. She looked into Dieter's wide eyes that revealed wisdom for his six years of age, "Thank you, Dieter."

"When be our stew?" he asked in a small voice, again returning to the innocence of his youth.

Anna wrapped her arms around her little brother, and sighing gently, said, "Soon, Dieter, soon."

***

The next morning, Anna found herself reluctantly walking up to where Sieghart and the strangers set their caravans for camp. The caravans in a half-circle, competed the circle with their tents, leaving a single gap as the only access. Entering camp, Anna noticed, in the middle, a modest campfire smoldered with a pot already set to heat. A handful of men sitting around the campfire or on top of the caravans drew Anna's attention. Observing so many men at leisure, other than her family or the occasional guest, made Anna suddenly feel uncomfortable.

In the coolness of the early day, with winter close, Anna hugged herself to keep warm. A simple breeze blew the flames of the visitors' campfire this way and that with an occasional flare or pop.

From among the men sitting around the fire, Sieghart watched Anna's approach and rose up to greet her. He noticed a grimace on her face and must have realized the awkwardness she felt. He spread his arms in welcome.

"Come, Miss. We've little, but it be ours, and it be ours to share!" he exclaimed, walking up to her and gesturing at the pot. While placing a blanket across her shoulders, he paused, with a smile in his voice, "But we took the liberty to put the water pot over the fire."

"It be no wonder ye needed a good cook, ye left your mothers at home, I see," she chided, while looking into the steaming pot.

"Thankfully, nay man can burn water," she muttered as she looked around for food stuffs to put in this 'stone' soup. "Do ye suppose some of ye might have something to cook in this 'water?'" A few of the men chuckled, but her stern look quelled that, and they all in unison, without being asked, inched away from the fire, several scurried away to bring what they could to add to the soup; others just moved to find a different perch quite content to let her work. Sieghart, unmoving and quietly resting against a caravan wheel, asked her name.

"Why?" she asked curtly, her jaw clenched. "I would think me uncle Karl announced that yesterday."

"Well, I'd rather call you by name than 'hey girl.' And, besides, I have no recollection of that courtesy being passed on. Maybe ye could help me here," he said with a questioning turn of his face.

"Anna," she returned abruptly.

As she worked, she looked around at the reclining men. Some questioning awareness niggled at the edge of her thought. The question returned quickly, back to her memories of the previous day. Sieghart did not answer the question then, and he appeared to avoid the issue now. *Who were these men?* They didn't look like merchants or a troupe of singers or mummers. They dressed like common men and carried no visible arms, but even to her eyes, they looked like fighting men. One of them, a bearded man dressed in a commoner's tunic, not the livery of a soldier or bandit, took great care in hiding half his face from her. Before he could turn away, Anna, however, caught a glimpse of a long, brutish scar running from chin to ear. Only the face of a mercenary or a soldier might carry such a scar.

Her mind raced, remembering other stories of marauders and bandits from other villages. *Were these bandits, or maybe marauders, but why would these men even offer to pay? Wouldn't they just take whatever they wanted?*

Maybe they were deserters from the Landlord's guard? That seemed more likely, but if that were the case, giving shelter to deserters would spell Anna and Dieter's ruin as well if caught by the landlord of the local manor or his men.

"Yer thinkin' something," came Sieghart's voice.

Anna paused a moment in her stirring of the morning meal. Startled by his voice back into the present, Anna determined it would be a welcome fall day no matter the reasoning of this band of men. The sun, now just above the horizon and shining through the trees, felt warm and reassuring though the question from a day earlier brought her question to mind once again.

She looked up at him with clear eyes. "I be askin' again, who be you people?"

"Nothin' but common men and good folk," he said easily.

"That's what ye said yesterday, and it meant just as little then as it do now," she replied hotly. "I be not the child ye think ye can fool with lies and half-truths. Ye appear to be fighting men returning from some adventure, even if I see nay swords. Who be ye? What be ye? Deserters?" She quarried, her voice becoming a bit louder and more pointed at Sieg as she waved her spoon at him and those around her.

A sudden hush fell over the men. Immediately, she regretted her outburst. "I be sorry for that," she said, quietly admonishing herself. Now pressured to her place among the men by their careful but curious gazes, some clearly surprised, Anna worked in silence. Looking at Sieghart, however, he simply returned a soft yet winning smile.

"Ye be half right," he said, "but ye be wrong as well, for I do not lie. We be merely good folk who cherish God and abhor the mistreating of the poor or weak. Tell me, who 'tis who represents the common people or who hast ever stood up fer ye and yer farmstead?"

"Nay anyone but ourselves," Anna replied bitterly, still feeling the previous nonverbal rebuke.

"That be right, and nay anyone else can," said Sieghart before raising a finger. "Nay body can help the people, except the people themselves. We be those people."

Suddenly, she understood, now thinking *rebels*. "Ye be rebelling against the crown," she said, standing and releasing the strain in her back from stirring the soup pot.

Sieghart, stirred by the question, grinned wolfishly. "Aye! We be those who stand against them who oppress us, who fill their pockets from the weak and poor content to kill the spirit of man. We be the sword and bow of the masses…." The intensity of Sieg's fervor increased as the words began to come from his emotions. Its ferocity almost scared Anna—just almost.

He continued to talk, and Anna listened with deepening awe as she worked the stew absently. Somewhere along the line, her instincts for self-preservation gave way to her curiosity. A beast leashed since her youth came rumbling out as she listened. Sieghart spoke with magnetic charm; his words carrying the truth of things. Anna always believed herself to be a straightforward woman, blunt and practical. However, underneath the charm of his words, Sieghart professed a doctrine with which she could agree.

All her life, she wondered at the *why* of things. All her life, she wondered why the nobles could levy their taxes with such impunity when the wars came and why they forsook their people in times of need.

Occasionally, the powers-that-were, the sheriffs or their overseers, in manor towns, would send appointed officials for the census. Every time, these fine men would look at the ramshackle hell of the Symon farm, or any other's holdings and snidely threaten to list them as 'Thriving.' This made the farm holdings of the manor eligible for a wider margin of taxation. A flick of the quill could correct this disaster, but no signature ever came. She thought. *And then there was the church and the clergy?*

Anna wanted to speak. She needed to Speak. Facing Sieghart, she opened her mouth, and the unintended interruption sounded from her. "I recollect, each year, Karl, he'd slide a little somethin' to the official suggestin' he just label the homestead as 'Meagre.' These collectors would then be on their way a penny or two richer." The outburst embarrassed Anna once again. She looked back, deep into the pot of stew and stirred.

"Aha!" exclaimed Sieghart when Anna mentioned the phenomenon. "That be exactly the sort of thing I mean. We grow their crops, we work for their benefit, and they profit from us in every way they can. The nobles, the officials, the clergy, the merchants… they treat us as nothings. But we be men… and women," he added hurriedly. "Nay, we be not sheep, nor dogs, nor cattle. They have taken from us the works of our labor—the labor of the folk, not of petty-kings, bishops, and counts!"

"The clergy of the Holy Roman Church under our corrupt Pope Martin V, saying they be the direct line to God and no other can do so, and our equally corrupt Emperor King, Louis IV, enacts taxes in the form of 'indulgences,' or payment to pray for the remission of thy sins before God." Sieghart continued, now growing in fervor again. Though only speaking to Anna, his voice rose and fell, weaving the cause of those who followed him. All around could hear and agree with his discourse.

"Not only do people pay taxes fer their land to the manor, but ye also pay taxes to the clergy for prayers before absolution. All these taxes going to build armies and build grand cathedrals," his voice now becoming quiet. "Helping the poor and week ne'er found its way into their intentions."

Sieghart soon took a deep breath in the realization he was speaking to all who agreed. A silence and then a rumble of assent and discussion came from the men leaning on caravans or sitting around the morning campfire.

Embarrassed, "I am sorry fer the rant," he said to Anna. I get angry when I think 'bout the wrong under which people without means exist.

Anna, taking all this into her thinking, looked Sieghart in the eye, "So, for a moment, pretend ye be right, and I'll agree the crown and the clergy steal, and we be stolen from. Ye be right; we be treated as fools by the wealthy and the church. Even now, my brother works to pay off the debts collected by a man who does not even own our farm. However, tell me this, what do ye intend to do about all this stolen wealth, as ye put it? How will yer two-dozen men contend with this petty king, these corrupt counts, and those usurping clergy?"

"We fight them," Sieghart said promptly, then laughed at the incredulous look on her face, and continued, "but we do not fight fairly. Nay, that would be suicide, and yet, we intend to live, but all the power these 'great men' have rests on supply-chains and the transfer of riches. We disrupt these supply-chains; we break into their little chests; we burn the displays of their opulence."

"So, ye steal and vandalize," Anna said with a hidden smile, but in her heart, she realized something not felt in a long time—the faint, red tinge of fervor. A desire to hope quivered inside her. A desire to throw out the poverty built by the unjust.

"We steal and return that wealth to our poor and displaced," Sieghart replied seriously. "We vandalize, for their fancy ways be naught but a mockery, and we go further: we brawl, we slay, and we strive to bring low these wicked folk who've brought ruin to so many others," Sieg explained with a hint of righteous anger.

A knowing silence fell over all present. All glanced around, and in that moment, Anna knew she would find her passion here, with these people. Dieter would be with her, and Yakov would return to establish his place, too. The thought of keeping up the farm and helping her uncle Karl quickly squashed any romantic thoughts she might have. She would not go but give encouragement to the men who would.

Despite the intensity of the debate, the silence turned into hunger. The morning pot of stew smelled excellent. With a final, almost uncharacteristic flourish, Anna announced the meal, ready to eat. An eager cheer around the camp became a mingling of discussion and jostling of excitement. She wondered if she should leave. Smiling and feeling the camaraderie, she, being in the habit of serving food back at home, began to pour a ladle or two of the rich broth into the bowls as each passed by. Finally, her eyes focused on a bowl coming towards her, she raised the ladle to pour a healthy portion in the bowl. Sieghart grabbed her hand.

Surprised and frowning, she looked up at him with stormy eyes, seeking some acceptance. Assuaged by his earnest expression, she smiled.

"'Tis nay only a man's fight, Anna," Sieghart said sincerely. "There be space fer ye amongst us as well."

"Are ye mad? I have a life here. I have an uncle…"

"An idiot and a fool."

"…and a little brother," she finished, flushed. "He be still very young. A woman and a child have no place among rebels."

"Ye know, this remanent of men is nay the extent of our cause," Sieghart said quietly. "Our base camp includes women and even children. Folk from all levels of society who can do a myriad of tasks and who support the changes that will come.”

“And most likely, they be all mad and believe in an unobtainable fantasy,” Anna snapped, pulling her hand from his grip. “And why would ye think I might share this madness? Who told ye I might believe in yer mad cause?”

“I watched ye at yer farm, and now, as I spoke, I just know,” Sieghart smiled, leaning back against the caravan. “Take yer time to consider, but I think I know what ye’ll choose because ye’re dying here on this farm, very slowly, but dying, nonetheless. I think ye wish to make a difference, and I think ye would rather fight fer a cause than live fer no reason.”

She stepped back from him, thunderstruck by his honesty and how close he hit on her thoughts. For just a moment, she wondered whether she should slap him, instead she stood and looked into the eyes of this incredulous man.

Now challenged by the feelings she knew for the cause, the responsibilities of the farmstead and her family, and now someone else possibly in her life, she turned and left without a word. *To the farmhouse*, she thought, breathing hard.

Entering the house, she found Dieter crying silently in the corner, his forehead bleeding. Eyes wide, she rushed to him with a yelp.

“Dieter? What happened, my sweet? What happened?” she asked, panicked.

"Broke my jug," came Dieter's small and weak voice. Anna turned around to see Karl in a drunken stupor half leaning from the doorway, a strange, angry grimace on his face, and holding his closed fist before him. He opened the fist to reveal shards of the glass jug, letting them fall to the floor as he stumbled in front of her, the palm of his hand, lacerated by small cuts and bleeding. "The little… he broke my best beer-jug. What boy breaks a man's beer-jug… a fine jug?"

"Ye mad drunk!" she screamed. Karl's expression clouded for a moment, and snarling, he raised his hand—then lowered it, blinking.

"Oh, but y're a fine girl, Anna," he said from his stupor. "Don't spoil the boy, don't spoil him. He broke my jug. Wha' boy… why, my father would have…" And muttering, he left the room as if forgetting his meaning.

"He broke it," Dieter said in a barely audible whisper, still sobbing. "He… drinking. Then… he threw it."

Holding her crying brother in her lap Anna sat quietly. She knew one thing. Sieghart was right. If she did nothing for the family, her mother's grave might soon have company.

Chapter VII: The Chain

"Men are born free. This we know; it is the gift of the Lord that we come to Earth with our own wills...

...But here on earth, we are bound. We are locked in the [pursuit of] gold or glamor, or the lust for wine or women, Lord save us... And are we not forced to live and die for others? We are brought to fire. We are brought to war.

We came here from innocence and found only chains."

-Unknown Monk, circa 1383

The timber-framed houses of the town of Helmstedt shone with rich melancholy under the heavy skies that hung over the town like the wings of some great angel. Rain or snow filled the dark clouds that rolled in each day from the east, but never dropped their wet blanket of white. A bitter chill permeated the air. Through biting cold whipped by wind, the eager supervisor did not stop forges from being lit, and in this, tired workers continued. Warmth radiated all around them as they stoked the fires, but the mindless manufacturing continued. The heat brought no comfort. This insane world, this new idea of profit, ran on the sweat of the poor.

Life in Helmstedt, like many other towns, depended on the Hanseatic league. A complex interconnection of trader's guilds, workshops, and trade alliances stretched from the frigid northern lands to the enigmatic lands of the Rus'. Timber, salt, silver, amber, and men travelled to and fro like blood in the veins of some gargantuan creature, and the economic integration meant great things for a few—though the decisions of the few meant a great deal for many more.

The women drew cold water from the wells, used by the smiths to cool the iron horseshoes. Then, in turn, horseshoes could be used by the caravans trading timber to produce crosses, pews, and spear hafts. Craft-houses, half warm, half frigid, clanged and scratched with the busy hum of production. In one such craft-house, Yakov watched with fascination the creation of a large cross. A balding, hawk-eyed man slowly carved the likeness of a crucified Christ ever so slowly, while a wisp of a boy handed him his tools. Adding another curve to Christ's eye, the man, tanned and leathery from constant work in all conditions, turned to look at Yakov from his work bench.

"Aye, now, prithee, don't jus' stand gawkin', speak!" he barked. "What task hath Adelman brought afore me? He pays me a mere pittance for me toil, and doth he expect me to reckon he sells it all in Saxony? Me young apprentices tell me they've glimpsed me handiwork as distant as Utrecht!"

Yakov opened his mouth to speak, only to be silenced by another tirade. Finally, the man waved his hand. "Go on, convey this to Adelman for me. I be needin' a guilder beyond the usual, or there be no pact 'twixt us!"

"But, Sir," Yakov said with a smile. "He's tossin' in a fresh guilder, be he, and addin' two groschen to sweeten the pot."

The man glared at Yakov as if some dire news lay hidden in the barter; then, with a cantankerous "Pah!", he turned back to his work.

"So I can tell me master..." Yakov ventured delicately.

"Aye, aye; his merchandise shall be ready as promised. Yet do inform him that me craftsmanship merits a dwelling beyond Utrecht. And if he cannot vend it yonder, then he be a daft swine, not a true merchant!"

With a patient smile, Yakov counted out the appropriate Witte, a silver coin used by the hanse in trade, and handed it to the merchant. The merchant eyed it carefully for the appropriate minting. Finishing the transaction, Yakov quickly made his final run of the day. Half the time he had worked here, Yakov had never known exactly what his job was; he was an every-job boy, one of the many employed by Adelman. Ambivalent to most of the time to the tasks given him, Yakov never knew exactly what his position involved.

This last run of the day took him to the outskirts of the town, to help with loading a wagon due to arrive in the afternoon. That done, Yakov found himself short of breath. He dragged himself back to Adelman's principle base of operations—a large, sloping tavern near the center of the town, and leaned briefly against the door post.

The only change Yakov experienced in the two months with Adelman came in the form of one change of clothes. In turn Mikkel, Yakov's friend, spent some of his hard-earned pfennig, the almost worthless pennies in the turning economy, on two tattered caps and marginally warm boots to ward off the seemingly never ending cold. He slipped through the dark doorway, his boots tracking snow into the musty establishment. Yakov and Mikkel, usually together, weaved their way through beggars, merchants, whores, and cavalrymen, and clambered up the ladder to the top floor of the tavern.

There, counting his money by the fire like a dragon, they found Adelman himself, an utterly unremarkable man dressed in a warm robe. Contrary to Karl's description, Adelman was neither fat nor ugly; however, he did have a straight, long beard, unaccompanied by any whiskers. On his head sat a fur-rimmed, pointed hat that folded down to fall on his shoulder. Casually pushing a small fortune in silver groschen coins aside, he fixed his sharp eyes on Yakov as the boy entered.

"Share with me some tidings. Young Yakov," he said with a sly grin. "make it a pleasant report, mind ye."

Yakov took a deep breath. "The wagon with the amber is coming in from the south in around a fortnight. It is intact and un-accosted. The Slav merchant will bring in good ornaments of true elk-bone—nothing pagan. All according to the will of the Holy See." Yakov continued, panting for breath. "He'll get them wares in a brace of days, mayhaps three if the snows do fall. We lent a hand to the stable master down yonder in the southern barn tendin' to the foals. The head of the woodworker's guild, he's struck a deal for a fresh guilder and a pair of groschen. And as for the caravan, she be all loaded up and ready to roll." Yakov, now finished, took a deep breath and exhaled heavily.

Adelman's expression did not waver throughout the report, and once Yakov finished, the merchant gave him his usual nod and returned to counting. As Yakov turned to leave, another boy entered, his shaking hands stiffly by his sides. Their eyes met, and Yakov quietly ducked out of the room knowing the boy was about to report something less than satisfactory.

***

A half-hour later, as Yakov and Mikkel warmed themselves by the fire downstairs in the tavern discussing their deliveries of the day, the boy descended from the ladder to the upper floor. His face was bruised and swelling from a clout by one of Adelman's guards. The others immediately made space for him. The boy sat by the fire, wordlessly gazing into its flames. Yakov shuddered. He'd never seen it, but everyone knew Adelman could be cruel, a side that revealed itself rarely—but fiercely.

Adelman never beat the boys himself, of course. He hired professionals to mete out discipline. Adelman used paid professionals to take care of his darker requirements and keep the boys in line.

Jon and Ingmar, two of those hired professionals, came to the tavern occasionally, to drop more debt-money off to Adelman and receive new assignments. Yakov and Mikkel knew them well. A clatter of horses came from outside and the jingle of tack and the voices of armed men. The two boys turned expecting Jon or Ingmar to enter. Instead, a stranger, clad in dark, badly oiled mail and a grimy surcoat entered the creaking door. He gave the boys by the fire a grim glance and climbed up the ladder to Adelman's loft.

Mikkel stared at the stranger as he climbed. Then before looking at Yakov and the others, he whispered. "He had his eyes fixed on us, he did. What's his gaze aimed at, I wonder?"

"Ye be readin' too much in a glance, Mikkel," said Günter, another of Adelman's boys, the oldest among them. T'were just a look, nothin' more."

"He be a stranger," Mikkel protested. "Why'd he fasten his gaze upon us? None usually spare us a glance."

"Mayhaps Mikkel has th'right of it," Yakov added, scratching flakes from his hair. "T'was a queer glint in his eye, as if he be…measurin' us up."

"Well, if you're so clever, why be ye toilin' here, payin' off some old man's debts? Seems like ye be the one playin' the fool in this tale."

Yakov's ears burned. Abruptly, he turned away. Mikkel looked at Yakov and Günter incredulously. Then, gently touching Yakov's shoulder, he asked, "You trust me," he reiterated. "Yakov, there be somethin' mighty queer about all this!"

"Y'be right," Yakov said, before angrily standing up.

"Where ye be goin', red-ears?" Günter yawned.

"T'see what be nay-right," Yakov said through clenched teeth before climbing up the ladder. He ignored the surprised hubbub from the boys behind him. Adelman would not brook unasked-for interruptions. Yakov, knowing a beating would be coming if caught, clenched his fists, and moved toward the hatch.

The door between the hatch on the upper floor and Adelman's quarters, usually ajar, was now shut. Creeping up to it on all fours, Yakov peered through a crack in the door and saw Adelman looking at a moleskin pouch. He weighed it in his hand and turned it once before looking at the armored man standing before him. "…But not sufficient for the whole lot of 'em, I'm afraid. I can't part with all me lads in the winter season."

"Oh?" said the man in a coarse voice. "But ye can find some other poor sods, nay?"

"Easily."

"Then spare a thought for our holy Bishop," the man said, leaning on Adelman's elm desk. "He'd hear of yer kindness, and he's a rightly kind man to his friends."

Adelman looked at him, one eyebrow raised expressionlessly, then jingled the purse. "Too little for all me boys."

"Oh, aye—but it might be less," the man remarked, eying the numerous charts strewn upon Adelman's table. "We've heard tale of yer forthcoming cargo. Slavic craftsmanship, bone trinkets, amber, salt, and silver adornments, adorned with garlands. Sounds a bit heathenish, if ye ask me."

Yakov's eyes widened as he saw Adelman suddenly turn pale. "'Tis for winter feasts, ye know that. Even the church…"

"You'll be damned, ye fool," the man whispered harshly. "Refuse the Chain, and 'tis akin to defying His Most Holy Bishop. Reject His Exalted Eminence…"

The man's arm stretched and, spitefully, he crossed Adelman with his own hand.

"…An' ye say nay to the Church." The man finished, and Adelman shuddered visibly, before pocketing the pouch.

"'Twill suffice," he said stiffly.

"Make sure them lads be set by the morrow's morn." the man ordered, before turning, stamping loudly across the room, and leaving Adelman's quarters. Climbing down the ladder, he grabbed a surprised woman, kissed her, and then left the tavern with an uninterrupted, violent gait.

Sitting by the fire, Yakov shuddered, having barely escaped before the man opened the door. The boys gathered around him, looking at him in askance. Even Günter looked at him with badly disguised curiosity.

"Well Mikkel inquired with a touch of impatience. "What's the fuss about? Were we on the mark? Was he chattin' 'bout us?" Yakov nodded.

"What did he be wantin' with us?"

"Nay but us," Yakov shivered. "I think… I think they be wantin' t'send us t'war. I think mayhaps we jus' been sold to the His Most Holy Bishop."

***

The next morning, it began to snow.

Delicate snowflakes drifted in with the chilly wind. The boys shuffled off to the outskirts of town, led by Adelman himself and one of his daughters, Fraulein Lea. The boys walked with a despondent, dragging gait, knowing exactly where they were being led thanks to Yakov.

"Be this necessary, father?" Lea asked her father suddenly. Lea, the only one of her sisters who lived with her father, would occasionally sneak leftovers from their table to give to the boys.

As Yakov watched silently, Adelman gave her an emotionless look. "Ye must be thinkin' with yer mind, daughter," he said plainly. "Nay with yer heart."

"Aye, father," Lea said quietly, and that ended the discussion.

As he walked alongside Yakov, Mikkel gave him a nudge. "I nay be seein' Günter here."

"He likely tried to make a run fer it," Yakov muttered, weariness in his voice.

"What do ye mean, 'make a run fer it'? Maybe he succeeded," Mikkel hissed. "We should run too."

"He couldn't escape here," Yakov said with grim certainty. "Everybody knows everybody. Nay a thing be unnoticed."

Mikkel grew quiet, and soon they reached their destination, a place known to the locals as Old Man's Rest. Underneath a sprawling, almost abnormally large maple tree, stood a mostly abandoned sentry post—little more than four posts holding up a roof of spaced wooden beams, intended to hold thatching. Several men sat near small fires, warming their hands, sometimes quietly talking, sometimes just…silent.

Empty from thatch, however, the structure stood barren, aside from a a tarp half-thrown atop the sentry post, making a makeshift pavilion. Underneath sat a man on a chopping block. He worked steadily on a war-hammer with a single-handed haft, polishing it until it reflected the dancing fire of the pit.

Tall and imposing even as he sat, he displayed more muscle on him than fat. Short, close-cropped red hair covered his head, and his sunburnt, leathery face shone beardless in the firelight. The wrinkles of his skin curved in the manner of a man used to grinning. His eyes were dark and hooded, sunken into the shadows of his jutting brow. He watched the boys' arrival with a wide grin formed across the shadows of his face. He wore no armor on his body except a sleeveless vest of dark chainmail, bound to his body by a belt. Around him, half-armored men stood or sat idly, some sharped spearheads, or some ate lukewarm gruel.

Already the new recruits—unarmed, wide-eyed youths—collected before the man. Adelman directed Mikkel and Yakov to join the group. Adelman then stepped back and at his instructions, these new men and boys stood to attention while the red-haired man inspected them.

Yakov saw a figure come up to them. It was the man who visited the tavern the day before, and he gave each of the boys a cold look. Then he turned and faced Adelman.

"One be missing," he stated.

"He took off," Adelman stated coolly, "I dispatched one of me men to fetch him back, but he got a bit... too eager. The lad won't be walkin' again, I'm 'fraid. He's hardly of much use to *me* now, let alone to ye."

"We paid ye for the lot," growled the man. "Your lapse be nay any fault of ours. We require all the --"

"Leave it, Roland," the red-haired man said loudly. Abruptly, the man stopped. Roland's quiet helper fixed his gaze on Adelman.

"Do ye know who I be?" he asked.

Adelman matched his gaze. "Yer name be Petres. Yer the one called 'the Chain'."

The knight grinned, and it reminded Yakov of a dog baring its teeth. "Indeed, y'speak true. I'd say I'm sorry for this disruption, but I've always had a disdain for merchants. I've always deemed them..." He paused, a wicked glint in his eye. "Pathetic! Aye, that's the very word." He straightened and breathed deeply, his nostrils widening as he looked around the camp.

He spoke in a singsong voice. The barest hint of an accent followed his words. Adelman stiffened at his words but ignored them in his reply. "Now, I've brought ye these boys and-"

"Men," corrected Petres, staring at the boys with the same grin. "Ye've brought me men, fighting men!"

"Boys, men, whichever," Adelman continued with annoyance creeping into his voice. "A few of 'em have been laboring to settle their debts. What be yer plan fer dealin' with that matter?"

Petres waved his hand. "Ye'll acquire whatever earnings they muster in their absence. They ain't chattel, mind ye! I merely secure these wayward lads a fresh, worthy master. In due course, I'll dispatch a man to scrutinize your records."

Adelman glared at him coolly, one eyebrow raised, then gestured to his daughter. As they turned to leave, Petres called him. "Merchant!"

Adelman turned around, only to see knight make an obscene gesture at him. A smattering of cackles rose among the assembled men. Flush with rage, the merchant put his arm on his daughter's shoulders and quickly walked away.

Petres, hooting with laughter himself, stood up and walked over to the new recruits. He rested his war-hammer on his shoulder. Cleverly wrought, the size of a fist on one end, shortening to a point on the other, he pointed the haft at each of the boys as he paced.

"I spun a web of deceit fer that merchant," h chuckled darkly, his smile unnerving. "Ye lads ain't men yet, nay, not yet. But I'll forge ye into men, y'bastards, and if I don't, I'll see ye meet yer end like men! What more could ye possibly wish fer?"

Petres paused and looked at them with suddenly sinister, deadly eyes. "Should ye possess mothers, fathers, brothers, sisters… banish them from yer minds. Yer mother be naught but muck, and yer father, a river of gore! Muck and gore, that be the measure of a man!"

Mercenaries of Petres the Chain's guard, standing around or leaning on posts of tents, muttered agreement while the recruits blanched and stood, eyes roaming from face to face in bewilderment.

"Why, don't just gawk there like addled owlets, ye fools!" Petres bellowed, exasperated. "Squat up and down, as if the gripes have seized you like a proper man! There! Up and down, you sluggish wretches. Up! Down!"

Yakov squatted up and down with dead eyes. *I don't care what ye say,* he thought. *I have a family, and I will go back to 'em.*

"They be waiting fer me." He murmured "I will go back. *I-"*

Suddenly, he felt a sharp pain in his gut, and he doubled over, retching. Something was sticking into his gut. Looking down, he saw Petres' foot. Crumpling, he groaned as the Chain looked down at him, nothing in his face but malice. The Chain's war-hammer lowered slowly. The cold metal pressed against Yakov's cheek as he tried to breathe.

"I glimpsed it in them eyes," the Chain uttered, the frigid metal pressing harshly against Yakov's jaw. "Ye reckoned ye could defy, but a man's gaze doth always expose him! Ye grasp it, ye filth. Ye fancy yerself untethered, but true freedom be but a fleeting dream. I'll ensure that ye—along with the lot of ya!—" he bellowed, "shall ne'er taste true freedom" And those words echoed ominously in Yakov's mind.

Ne'er be free.

Somehow, the words hurt him more than the pain.

Chapter VIII: River's Edge

"Good men come to God, gold, or grief, but they begin with gentle hearts and dreams."

-Unknown Monk, circa 1384

Reflected light danced iridescent on the freshly fallen snow of the previous night. Under the clear blue sky, the chill air stood as still as a mountain. Tendrils of steam escaped from Anna's mouth, swirling pale like the wispy clouds passing overhead. She and Sieghart watched, frozen in the moment with the anticipation of the hunter on the track of a meal to come. The only movement came from a stream a short distance away, which forced its way over boxy rocks and around serpentine bends, making its way through a labyrinthine of blockages.

Without warning, startled by a sudden appearance, Anna winced. Darting over the snowy knoll and along the bank of the stream, a rabbit abruptly changed direction and then jerked short under a frozen pine, its foot caught in the unforgiving embrace of a loop trap. Powdery snow flew in all directions. The animal's loud squealing became higher in pitch as the hare tried to escape. The noose, taut now, would not yield its prey. Watching the struggle, Anna could only feel a deepening pity for the small creature.

After half an hour of fruitless struggle that kicked up clouds of powdery snow, the hare quieted enough for Anna and Sieghart to approach. Hushing the small animal as she moved in, Anna intended to finish the work afoot quickly. Stooping down, she caught the squirming hare between her knees while holding it down with her offhand. Using a knife, she clutched in the opposite hand, as shown by Sieghart, she dispatched the creature with one quick stroke across its throat. A childish innocence in her heart felt a pang of remorse, though the feeling became quickly quashed by hunger.

"Well caught," called Sieghart, half leaning against a tree. He munched an apple, now smiling at her, her face expressing both the sorrow and elation of the moment. He wore his tattered, quilted waistcoat that flared from his broad shoulders. She blushed.

"We used to lay hare-traps in the copse 'round the farm in winters," she muttered as she pulled the surprisingly heavy hare from the looped rope.

"Mayhaps I can give ye a bit of help," Sieghart spryly bounced over a fallen log, clearly eager. Shooting him a menacing glance, she permitted him to pick up their quarry. He grinned. "Would ye be up to goin' back t'camp with me?"

"I've yet a bucket to be fillin', I do."

Sieghart waved his hand dismissively. "Leave it be; I'll dispatch someone later. We've got more than enough water fer now."

Sighing, Anna walked back to camp with Sieghart. The camp, well disguised, lay in a large, depressed hollow formed by the stream, which looped down a hill, gouging out its banks to expose old, snow-bright rocks. Behind a shroud of dry, frosted shrubs and a half-fallen tree was the hollow sheltered by a hilly crag of rock. This made an ideal place to camp, quite spacious and—most importantly, for men and women, on the run—covert.

Two scrawny men sat, rough-bearded and hawkeyed, on a log in front of some bushes guarding the encampment. Putting their bows away as Sieghart and Anna appeared, they gave curt nods to Sieghart before blowing warmth into their hands. Ratty shawls looped around some heads, like turbans of the Musselman from the crusade-lands; they protected their ears against the harsh cold.

Now, moving beyond the scratching shrubs, narrow trail, and haggard guards, a collection of tents spiraled out from a central fire, large and cheery. A quick look around the camp revealed smaller fires scattered about. Warming themselves around the fires, men, and even some women, poked the flames or stirred a pot to prepare some palatable soupy stew. A man with a turban sat nearby, arranging a collection of pinecones. Next, after placing embers into one of the heating pots, he put pinecones, one by one, on the embers. Cackling to himself with amusement, the cones popped and cracked. Finally, pulling hot seeds from the peddles, wincing as he ate, he smiled widely with satisfaction.

"Don't burn your tongue, Kaspar," Sieg laughed, walking past, with Anna close behind. Kaspar, a man with more hair than sense, shot Sieg a bucktoothed grin and went back to gleefully popping pinecones.

A part of the group in general for only a few weeks, Anna looked around, beginning to feel the unfamiliar warmth of welcome. Though strange as the feelings might be, the camp, which they reached just this week, felt homely. Amazement befell her, for of all the things she imagined about rebels, this camp's acceptance broke any story or myth told her by leaders of her community. *These folk, they jus' be wantin' to cling to life in a world where their own kings and bishops have turned 'gainst 'em,* she thought. *Nay soldiers nor hired blades, but 'tis a heavy burden they bear, all prayin' fer a chance t'go back to their humble farms and shops in peace, one day.*

Anna observed the women in camp washed clothes and looked after the odd child as just a part of the group. Beyond the child-rearing and domestic chores, little difference appeared between the work of the men and the women. They all gathered, hunted, and fought when need be. Anna noticed a practicality about the community also. When some were away, others picked up the responsibilities left behind. Everyone pitched in without too many grumbles. She admired the warmth of comradery for survival among the group's members. A welcoming blanket of hope now pressed close in around Dieter and her. Once again, she felt warm.

Sieghart's voice quickly brought Anna back from her reverie. "Rejoice, gentlemen!" Sieghart called as they neared the central fire.

Her face burning, Anna elbowed him in ribs—too late she realized—a boisterous cheer rose from all those half-frozen rebels before her. Anna, carrying the freshly killed hare by the ears, smiled back, her red cheeks accenting her embarrassment. A warmth, as if home, from these unshaven men and harried women brought her quickly into their commune as a sister. *It is home.* Anna smiled. *Yes. A new home.*

From the opening in a nearby low hide-covered hut, Anna noticed movement. Awareness coming quickly, and a bit taken aback, she recognized Dieter as he crawled out from the heavily drooping tent. Red-nosed and wheezing a bit, he looked like a bear emerging from hibernation. With ratty shawls, worn waistcoats, and torn scraps of warm cloth, the new commune of friends ensured to keep him safe and warm until Anna's return. Anna gathered him to her for a few minutes before she assured herself he felt improved. She smiled and surrounded him with a heartfelt embrace.

With pomp, Sieghart presented the dead hare to Dieter, who peered over Anna's arm at it with a child's puzzlement.

"Yer sister caught 'em fer us, little man," Sieghart chuckled, speaking with a voice all could hear. With one eye open, Dieter looked at Anna questioningly. "Dinner will be a fine-grand affair," Sieghart joked. All cheered again. Dieter yawned once more and settled into Anna's warmth.

"Us?" Dieter asked.

"Aye!" Sieghart smiled assumingly with a questioning look at Anna. Reassured by her stubborn blush, he turned back to Dieter. "This be yer home now."

Anna returned a veiled smile, then bent down to tousle Dieter's hair. Dieter yawned widely. Anna, Looking at Sieghart, motioned meaningfully toward the tent.

"Dieter ought to be tucked in slumber; he should," she said, hoping he would take the hint. Comprehension dawned in Sieghart's curious eyes.

A moment of nervous silence passed between Anna and Sieghart. A realization turned into a sudden reaction by Sieghart. "Ah...aye. Come through."

With Dieter between them, they entered the tent. A small but relatively warm space, full of warm cloths, tattered furs, and old hay, it reminded Anna a little of a bird's nest, a private sanctuary for the three of them.

"Did ye want to talk?" Sieghart finally asked as Anna helped Dieter back into his bed.

"I did." Seated next to Dieter, she brought together her will and focused her thoughts. Raising her head and looking directly into Sieghart's eyes. "Ye said ye'd send word to Yakov," Anna quarried, trying not to let panic into her determined voice. "Might we have received word by now?"

"Well," he said, sighing an exhale of silent surrender. "Aye, some news has come." He paused. He moved to his mostly empty chest tucked into a corner of the tent and sat down. His lanky legs crossed, he leaned forward with both hands bracing against his thighs and reported the unfulfilling news to Anna.

Sieghart paused and cleared his throat as if reluctant to give a full account, but then continued, "Aye… one o'them messengers be 'bout to show up any time. Seems our sentries stumbled 'pon that fool, half-starved and nay far from this place. He's bringin' us the goods we need, but his horse dropped dead fer the lad ridin' it so hard. He a greenhorn, bein' excited and all, makin' his first blunder."

Anna showed concern but then asked impatiently, "So, aye, all said and done, be there a message delivered to the sentries?

"Our messenger, good lad he be, bein' kept at the guard post, won't let 'im go 'til he's ate and proper rested." Sieghart answered. "He's got some news fer us, Anna, see, but insisted on givin' it t'me face-to-face. So, we bide our time—reckon he'll show up 'fore long." He paused in thought, looking into Anna's eyes, "Mayhaps jus' patience will suffice for a short period."

Anna nodded, still worried. She sat in thought, wondering about this rag-tag outfit that was simultaneously a well-run machine of diverse individuals. The group's communication connections and intelligence gathering consisted of an elaborate yet rigid system of riders, listeners, scouts, and messengers. This mystified Anna. The fascinating yet beautifully elaborate system, with its many logistical parts, made the elusive group's leader, der Flechtemann, a masterful genius.

"Tell me about him," she blurted out, now turning red with embarrassment in reaction to Sieghart's surprised laugh.

"Him who?" he asked, amused.

"Thy leader," she said crossly, trying not to let her embarrassment show too much. "Der Flechtemann."

Sieghart simply stared at Anna as if looking right through her. His cheerful eyes shifted from her questioning face to Dieter. Dieter now given in to the sand of sleep breathed easily, snugged into his bed...in his new home.

"He be a great man, aye," Sieg murmured, "...der Flechtemann."

"Why 'great?'"

"He jus' puts it plain," Sieghart remarked. "Folks tend to see 'im as distant—rightly so—he's out in them fields most days. But let me tell ya, he's got a deep, burnin' care, he does. He looks out fer us, his comrades, and all the regular folds. There be a genuine warmth in his heart, a rare sight in these tryin' times."

"Ye talk like he be some harmless monk."

"Oh no," Sieg laughed. "Nay, very far from harmless, and certainly no monk—he'd frown on such likenin', for sure," he reflected. "But mark me, there's a love deep in his heart, even if he be short-spoken, even if he be choosen the path of bow and sword. His fierceness ain't without purpose. It ain't 'bout himself nor driven by greed. He don't relish the torment, not even if them noble folk who'd love to see 'im strung up if they could. "Tis a cruel jest, they bein' called 'nobles' and him the outlaw, in my reckonin'."

Anna understood his point. Any man who could create a band of rebels so humane as the one around her could not do so without having a true streak of idealism. They weren't a hoard of undisciplined murderers; they had a firm hold over their own humanity, over the very essential parts of what made a man good.

"Sounds like he be a fine leader," Anna said, hesitating. "But I can't help but wonder why he ain't among us, leadin' his troops. Where might he be, if not here with us?"

Sieg folded his arms. "Der Flechtemann, he ain't no highborn lord, but he leads by showin' the way. In his own speakin', he ain't even our chief, just a fella put in place to look after us. He's out there most times with the scouts, throwin' himself right into harm's path for the sake of the ones trustin' in him. We've said it, and I've said it to 'im plain—it's too perilous. He should let the lads handle it themselves. But he pays us no heed, as expected."

It seemed strange to Anna that a leader of any sort would claim to be serving the men following him. She said as much to Sieghart, who shook his head.

"I held the same thinkin' fer the longest spell," he said. "Yet now, it's dawnin' on me. If he ruled us with a heavy hand, what'd set him apart from them corpulent old gents we strip of their ill-gotten gains? He's got nay fondness for the kind who send others to their graves while they sit comfy. He's always held to the notion folks should have a voice in who leads 'em."

"Like elders at a dispute," Anna said, making the connection. Traditionally, any disputes regarding land between landowners, neighbors, or any two parties in the countryside would be resolved by a meeting of trusted elders from the homesteads and villages nearby. These elders, agreed upon by all involved as being trustworthy folk, would meet at one of the villages, or at a family's homestead, and resolve any disputes.

"Aye, exactly!" Sieg exclaimed. "Among us regular folk, we've always reckoned that be the only sensible path— lettin' yer choices be decided by men ye can rely on. But what them nobles been up to? They've plopped themselves in high seats, all by their lonesome, propped up by riches instead of honor. If ye inquire of me, they're akin to leeches, feastin' on…"

At that moment, the shaggy mane of one of the men popped into the tent, and he looked Sieg and Anna apologetically.

"Sorry fer interrupting," he muttered indistinctly before looking at Sieg. "That fool scout from Helmstedt just showed up. Y'coming to meet 'im, or…?"

"Nay, show him in," Sieghart said easily. "The matter concerns the Fräulein in any case."

Anna waited anxiously as the man nodded and left. She looked at Dieter, who now lay fast asleep a result of listening to the elder conversation. She checked his forehead and sighed in relief to find it only lukewarm instead of hot.

Then the tent-flap was slipped aside as a bony-looking man crept inside, wearing two layers of wool, his dark beard still grimy with food-grease. His eyes flitted between Sieg and Anna as he nodded nervously.

"At ease, man," Sieg sighed. "Ate well?"

"Aye, sir."

"Planning t'override any horses in the future?"

"Nay, sir."

"Good man," said Sieg with an encouraging smile. "Now, give me your report. How does our dear Anna's brother fare in old Helmstedt?"

"I bear grim tidings, Miss," the scout uttered, lowering his head as Anna's heart sank. "Yakov, that be Yakov Symon, has been pressed into the wars."

"Conscripted?" Anna burst, her voice shrill in panic. "He be jus' a child! He… he can't…"

"Which army?" Sieg asked, frowning at the scout.

The scout gulped. "Mercenaries, sir—the Chain's lot, though I reckon they've be hired by some noble to take up spears."

"Hold…" Sieghart charged, "The Chain? *Petres* the Chain?"

"The very selfsame, sir," the scout responded. "I reached the place on the very day they snatched 'em away. I tried a quick pursuit, hopin' to catch the merchant ere they handed the lads to them hired swords—but I was too late. I stumbled upon the merchant and his daughter, but it be as they be headin' back from the mercenary camp. I took a peep at it too, sir, but there be too many blokes. Tryin' to spring him loose would've been nothin' short of suicide fer us both."

"Nothin' ye could've managed, nay 'gainst that gang," Sieg grumbled, running his hand through his hair in distraction. "By the heavens, did it have to be that brute Petres?"

Anna looked ahead numbly. Her brother, her little brother, had been taken to fight in some godforsaken war—her little brother? But only last year, she was combing his hair for lice, scolding him for this thing or that, sending him off to do his chores. His half-moon, childish face appeared before her mind, and try as she did, she could not imagine him carrying a sword, or a spear, or a buckler.

"Anna?" came Sieg's voice, and she snapped out of her reverie, looking at him with wet eyes.

"I warned 'im to take on his duties," she murmured softly. "I advised him to go there, and now he be…Oh Lord, he won't endure a war. He be but a wee one—why did I n're see how small he truly be? He seemed more a lad than a grown man. He couldn't… I jus'…"

"There, there," Sieghart spoke soothingly, gently resting his hand on her shoulder as she wept. "He ain't that tender in years, nay—and he likely ain't bound fer the front lines, I'd wager. More like he'll find himself in a cozy ol' garrison somewhere… likely not too far up north either, so I reckon he won't be caught in any sieges. It'll turn out fine, aye? Hear me out, it ain't yer donin's…"

And though later she would appreciate his attempts at consolation, at that moment, Anna thought of nothing but her little Yakov, hair shorn like a soldier, blood streaking his face, eyes dead to the world.

Chapter IX: Blood and Iron

"...but there are so many ways of doing the same things. There is inspiration that strikes the heart from the pen of the well-intentioned. There is the honest effort of principled men. There is the good sense that comes from [mutual] agreement and consultation...

But O fool, you seek success through means other than these excellent ways. The bright spear, the bloodied ax... your love is perverse, for you love blood and iron."

-Unknown Monk, circa 1384

In the shadowy sunset, among trees providing an early evening, an older soldier mended a chainmail coif by bending chain links together, creating a scar from a clean cut in the mail where an axe had ended the owner's life. His work finished and admired; he threw the coif to Yakov. With a curious eye, he waited for Yakov to understand cleaning needed to happen. Yakov, wearily understood the gesture, sat on a fallen log, oiled, and cleaned the coif with a greasy rag. He tried not to wretch as he pulled at strands of hair clogged with blood matted between the chain links. The bald mercenary stood nearby and chuckled at Yakov's discomfort.

"Happens sometimes, y'see," he said in a hoarse voice as Yakov continued to clean and oil the chainmail hood with feigned eagerness. "That particular piece was yanked off a stiff, y'see, and well, the hair and hide sometimes comes along for a ride, a-times."

Yakov felt his stomach churn at the thought but held his gorge back with quiet reserve, trying not to show emotion as he finished the coif. Still chuckling, the bald mercenary picked up the coif and, nestling it over his head, slapped Yakov on his back, and left. Yakov sat still, watching the mercenary walk away. Then, looking at the camp around him, night slipped over the rays of the sun; bonfires shone brighter; an owl's screech in the distance announced the stillness of night.

Mikkel appeared from the dark shadows with deep circles under his eyes and sat down beside Yakov quietly. He carried a bundle of clothes, which Yakov eyed then glanced askance toward his friend.

Drawing himself up a bit, and trying not to give Yakov a wrong impression, "I helped sew up some gambesons," he said quickly, returning Yakov's glance and then examined his fingers, covered in needle-pricks and cuts. "One's fer ye, one's fer me."

"It be jus' cloth," Yakov frowned, then covered a smile, picking up the gambeson shirt—a quilted, faded shirt-vest of patch-worked red and white. "Do ye think this really counts as armor?" he said, holding the garment up to the light.

Mikkel shrugged. "Some of the older lads say it helps against the sharp stuff—knives, swords, and the like. Axe or mace, though, and you're dead."

"Better'n nothin', I guess," Yakov mimed and slipped it on over his ragged wools. Though still loose, Yakov assumed he might grow into it with time. Already, since leaving the farmstead, Yakov sensed himself taller and possibly an inch or two wider at the shoulders.

"My my," came a voice. The voice of Petres the Chain startled the new recruits. Startled, Yakov and Mikkel could see the silhouette of Petres the Chain observing them, war-hammer on his shoulder, his eyes glinting in the dark like black jewels. "Looks like fightin' men a'ready—but nay, fightin' men don't have time to waste. Do they?" He said sarcastically.

Yakov and Mikkel moved their heads from side to side as they responded to The Chain's question, hesitation in their acknowledgement.

"Then be off to yer chores," The Chain roared with sudden ferocity. "Get going, and inquire what tasks await!" he bellowed, his voice dripping with malice. "See to it, ye idle wretches.!"

Ears ablaze with alarm, Yakov followed Mikkel as they scampered off to look for something else to do, hearing the Chain's laughter booming behind them.

***

The next few days passed in a blur. Or were they weeks?

Yakov and Mikkel, now fast friends, became wary of being caught idle anywhere. The other new recruits similarly split into ones and twos, and although they huddled over the same campfire and chewed on the same gruel, they were all too tired and distant to talk. *What be there to talk 'bout anyways?* Yakov would think. *We are where we are for now.*

Of course, not everyone agreed. At one point, one of the new lads, a gangly, jumpy youth named Hanno, attempted to escape. He planned it well enough. Creating an obvious trail through the undergrowth in one direction, he backtracked and escaped in the opposite. It was a decent plan—even the use of an animal's blood threw the searching guards off for a time; however, it didn't fool the pursuit entirely, but it should have slowed them down.

It did not. The moment the Chain was shown the trail, he sent two men in the opposite direction. In a few hours they returned, dragging the screaming youth by his ankles. As Yakov watched in mounting horror, the Chain took a dagger from one of the men with exaggerated politeness, grabbed Hanno roughly by the hair, and cut two wedges out of one of the youth's ear. One of the wedges, not cut completely through, hung limply by a thread of skin for a moment. The Chain sighed and pulled it off, showing the bloody piece to the rest of us as Hanno howled in anguish with deep sobs, blood running down one cheek and over his tunic.

"Next time one of ye gets any ideas," he said with a malevolent grin, "I'll skin the runt alive. Nay death for deserters, that be how I do it!"

Then, tossing the bloody piece of Hanno's ear nonchalantly into the campfire, the mercenary leader left. Yakov tried to swallow the bile down his throat as the men released Hanno, who fell, his hand over the cut ear, into a blubbering wreck on the dirty snow.

Over the next few days, they saw little of the youth. Hanno often sulked at the edges of camp, a long rag tied in a halo around his head to cover the raw mutilation of his ear. No one talked to him anymore, afraid to be seen associating with a would-be-deserter. Once, as Yakov filled water from a nearby stream, he saw Hanno's spindly form sitting nearby. Hanno raised a bony hand in a dubious greeting, and Yakov returned the gesture hesitantly before hurrying back to camp.

Occasionally, as supplies waned, the Chain would exhort needed supplies from nearby homesteads. Despite bitter protests, most farmers would eventually hang their heads as the Chain's men left with baskets full of produce. In time, during the mercenaries' wanderings near the foothills and cliffs of a snowy mountain, the small army found a farm that clearly covered sprawling acreage. A large house with sloping walls was sighted tucked up against a cliff in the mountainside, overseing those same fields. The Chain knew the owners to be the Kaufmann family, an extended family of hardy hill-men encountered by the Chain before, who had refused to give the mercenaries even a turnip from the family stores.

Displeased with having to negotiate with old man Kaufman, the Chain decided to act in a belligerent manner.

By the time Yakov and the rest of the new recruits arrived at the farmhouse, a scene of a carnage spread before them. Yakov and Mikkel stood at the fence, looking at the corpse of a red-haired man, his face a bruised purple, eyes open with bloodshot regret. One of the mercenaries pushed the two recruits towards the scene.

"Begin with the purse," he said with malicious intent.

Silently, without sharing a word or a glance, Yakov and Mikkel complied. Yakov held his nose as he picked at the corpse carefully, trying not to inhale the smell of fear which still permeated, even after death, the man's clothes, and body.

"You'd best acclimate to that stench, lad," the mercenary's voice taunted. "That foul reek is the scent of battle, and into battle ye be marchin'."

Tired and disgusted, Yakov found himself sitting beside Mikkel on a fence. The latter leaned against a post, bent over, hands on knees, dry heaving. Yakov looked glumly ahead, lost in thought. Now, he relished the wonderful smells of his own family farm—the fresh green scent of spring, the dusty smell of autumn, the smell of flowers, earthy hay, the musky scent of the mushrooms that sometimes sprouted after the summer rain. The smell, also, of his mother's hair, the smell of Anna's cooking…

Yakov took a deep breath, trying to hold back tears. The mercenary who had insisted Yakov go through Kaufmann's pockets reappeared, holding two slings over one arm and carrying a bundle of rags under the opposite. Looking at Mikkel's heaving form with amusement, he handed both slings to Yakov and hung the rags from the fence.

"The Chain doesn't trust ye with anything pointy yet, but we found some slings on the dead upstairs. In the commotion, one of our number got hisself a solid knock from a rock, and now the poor sod's got only one eye left," he chuckled, as if recounting an old joke. Pointing to the rags, he continued, "Them be fer carryin' your belongin's. On general march, ye'll be carryin' them tied to the haft of a spear or slung o'er yer back. Ye know how to tie 'em into a sling?"

Yakov nodded. He and his family used to tie slings on a post, which would be carried by two people during harvest time to help lug crops back to the barn for storage. Of course, using the ox and cart worked better, but the sling was not unknown to Yakov.

"Good," the man grunted, looking content. "Either of ye lot ever put a man in the dirt?" The two looked back to the mercenary with blank looks on their faces. "Killed 'em," he rejoined loudly.

Yakov startled. "No, never."

He grunted. "Animal?"

"Yes," Yakov replied after thinking for a moment. He once killed an aggressive stoat slashing into it with a sickle. The stoat would not stay away from the crops, he remembered. Yakov could still hear in his mind the yowling, bloody screams of the animal as he'd put it down.

"Good enough," the man said carelessly. "Same enough thing."

But was it so, the same enough thing? Yakov thought. *Nay, it couldn't be. Humans showed a spark in their eyes in life. Was that the soul? But then,* Yakov contemplated, *don't animals, too? I'd seen terror in the stoat's eyes, seen them cloud over in death. What be that, if nay a soul?*

Oh, but it couldn't be, he thought, turning over later in the night. *Obviously, it be worse to kill a person. Nay? But the corpses required by the mercenaries to ransack were as still and lifeless as a dead animal. Their vacant eyes be clouded over too.*

Curling up into a fetal position, Yakov told himself to stop thinking, shutting his eyes, and trying to dream without sleeping, or sleep without dreaming. Anything to get his mind off the bloated face of the red-haired corpse that stayed before his eyes like the afterimage of the sun.

*****

Over the next month, the Chain's mercenary guard drilled and drilled the new recruits. There was no formal structure to this process. The boys, for not yet men, were given clubs or long, bladeless spear shafts to use. Emulating the movements of the mercenaries who taught them skills, they laughed and cavorted, showing off, yet in this chaos, the boys began to show cunning and skill. Occasionally, during the training, one of the mercenaries, to make a point, would kick the shins of the trainees, constantly checking for balance and firmness in the position of their stance. The new recruits slowly became accepted by the men of the band as their prowess improved. Little by little, the young lads became accepted parts of the whole.

On one unusually mild evening, Yakov found himself blinking the sweat from his eyes as the march halted for the day. His cheeks, a grey pallor, now dimmed from their usual redness, gave his skin an even paler glow from the effects of the forced march. His hands and feet, sore, scarred, and calloused, added to the painful agony from over-used muscles and joints over the entirety of his body. Though sore from the march, stopping with the others to rest for the night would bring much-needed relief.

Yakov followed the Chain to the top of a low hill. Stopping, they looked out under the argent moonlight at the barren stretch of moorland glistening silver before them. This small hillock would be a good place to camp and post sentries if one did not mind being observed by any enemy. Yakov grinned with understanding. The hill, forming a defensible position amongst the flatness of the moors, did not bring fear of exposure to the Chain. This would be a good place to rest. The Chain's tactical decisions in carrying out this business of war no longer surprised the seasoned warrior in Yakov.

Looting corpses from the remnants of a battlefield a few days back, Yakov collected a tattered red belt and a short, brutish dagger, which he now stashed under his belt. The knife lay with no sheath. Looking around the corpses, no scabbard could be found, nor anything that he might use to hang the knife from his new belt. For now, wrapped the blade in an oil-soaked rag and tucked it into the belt at his waste. This would do until he could devise a better way to keep the knife safe. Aside from this added accessory, he carried his spear tied with a sling over one shoulder. His other sparse possessions, bundled in a bit of cloth torn from the tunic of an unfortunate warrior on the battlefield, now hung over one shoulder, continued under the pit of the other, and tied across his chest.

Mikkel, meanwhile, luck following him, found a halfway-decent arming cap to keep his ears warm, though he continued to worry whether it would give him lice. Mikkel alternately grabbed the hat from his head and searched it for the elusive louse. He would then replace it. Soon, scratching his head again, he would repeat the routine. This went on for some time.

"Give that t'me," Yakov said, exasperated with Mikkel's antics. Yakov took the cap and tossed it into a steaming pot of water sitting on the edge of a campfire nearby.

"Hey, that be mine," Mikkel yelled, trying to grab the hat back from Yakov.

"That, my friend, 'tis true, but now we will nay have yer lice be as friends too." Yakov smiled in reproach.

Mikkel, with quick hands, retrieved the cap from the pot and wrung it fiercely, water running in rivulets to the ground. With a long face, he removed himself from Yakov's side for a short time. Returning shortly, Yakov only smiled, and they both broke into laughter. Mikkel crammed the soggy arming cap back on his head, puckered his face into a squinch and smiled. Yakov slapped his friend on the back, laughed again, and the two of them settled down to find something to eat.

Some of the mercenaries nearby chuckled at the antics of Mikkel and Yakov. One of the mercenaries seated alongside some of the recruits threw two faded cloaks to the two friends. "You will need these tonight. At least they are in good shape and will give some extra warmth," he said.

"Thanks, friend," Yakov returned. Mikkel only nodded and smiled.

Yakov and Mikkel, hungry from the incident and appreciative of the gesture of the cloaks, turned to find any food available. Camp was now set for the evening, the two collected their wooden bowls each carried in their possessions and went to the pot hanging over the cook fire nearby. More tasteless gruel faced them. They smirked, but it would help them warm. The two sat together near a fire to ward off the chill.

"I ain't laid eyes on Hanno in a while now," Yakov said suddenly.

Mikkel looked at him oddly. "Which Hanno?"

"Hanno! That lad whose ear got clipped by the Chain. He be 'round, but," Yakov scowled, "I ain't crossed paths with him lately. Or maybe it been more than a bit."

Mikkel hesitated. "Yakov, he be…not here anymore."

"What?"

"They found 'im dead a week back," Mikkel said, shifting uncomfortably as he tried not to look at Yakov. "I thought ye knew."

Yakov sat quietly, remembering the image of Hanno waving at him by the stream. After a while, he spoke again. "What be the cause?"

"All 'twas said he be feeble. Dunno, mayhaps he took ill," Mikkel pondered.

Hanno, the frail youth, simply gave up. Yakov knew in the pit of his stomach this was true. Over time, Hanno grew pale, blue veins became noticeable on his arms and legs, his eyes wide and sad. Hanno began to lag behind the unit on marches, and the two friends would need to go back and bring him into camp. Yakov gazed into the distance, suddenly sober with the reality Hanno now became just another face in the sea of the dead Yakov discovered over each hill or around each corner in the road during the past few weeks. The mirth of the moment rushed suddenly away leaving what seemed to be an empty place in his pride. In stories of war, princes would ride on horses of gold, and there was honor to be had, but Yakov knew the truth now—behind the stories, behind the notions of honor, behind the glorification of blood and iron, only a hungry pit lived in the guts of each soldier. A pit so dark and deep no man could see its bottom, and to try was to fall.

Hanno fell. That was all.

Chapter X: Men of God

"I've never agreed to be called a man of God. Are we not all His children? ... So beware [a man] who proudly names himself a man of God, for he snuck upon that title for himself alone."

-Unknown Monk, circa 1382

Wealth flowed up and down the Elbe river—down into the many duchies inland, or up towards the Northern Sea, where traders with icy eyes and rugged faces paid good money for goods travelling through the Sanctum Romanum. A key part of the Hanseatic League in this apparently calm, yet economically vital region was the city of Magdeburg, which pulsed with the life and energy that eclipsed the workshops and smithies of Helmstedt.

Separated from one bank of the river by an old ford and a newer bridge, the city seemed to rise out from the earth like a collective of mushrooms in bloom, with the red-tile roofing, the mossy shingles, and the cold white stone giving the city a strangely surreal appearance from the distance. Clothing lines connected buildings like a complex web, and garments dyed in every conceivable color flapped in the evening's breeze. Willows hung dismally over the river like bent old crones, and children ran up and down the bridge as the Chain and his company made their way across.

After the portly guards at the gates checked the seal the Chain provided to them, a party of men was allowed into the city while the rest crossed back over the bridge to make camp on the other side of the shimmering river. The party entering the city included the Chain himself, his personal guard, and half the new recruits, which included Yakov but not Mikkel. Yakov exchanged a worried glance with Mikkel before they were allowed to enter, led inside by one of the guards.

As they made their way through the throngs of men and women going about their business or eyeing them suspiciously. The opulence on display before Yakov struck him with awe. Despite the hardships of the winter and the recent seasonal changes, the men of the city dressed well, and merchants walked openly with golden rings on their fingers. Women's dresses were brightly dyed, and a rainbow of dazzling ribbons brought beauty to the plaited hair of the ladies. Some more conservative maidens simply styled their hair with nets.

Food-stalls lined the narrow streets, selling common goods or hot bowls of sausage-broth for the winter. The presence of mules, used to draw everything from small carts to entire wagons, cramped the streets further. Yakov, irritated by the cacophony of sounds, wished the mules would stop adding to the confusion by their baying so piteously.

Winding now through a slum area, the band of recruits stopped before a building obviously under construction. The small area of crude shacks and the wreak of refuse in the pathways signaled the living quarters of the masons and common laborers in the construction crews who slept and passed away any idle time available. Even though the squaller abounded, the stonework of the incomplete structure, even to Yakov's inexperienced gaze, shone the mastery of the workers. To his eye, the walls were properly erect without sways or curves. They were tall with pleasing arches; however, Yakov could feel the imposition of piety saturate his senses. An unfinished bell tower with vacant windows where stained glass would someday allow daylight rays to dazzle participants identified the building as a cathedral.

Before the cathedral, a throng of churchmen stood, arguing amongst themselves. To Yakov's surprise, the gilded attire of these leaders of the church put the officiates of Helmstedt to shame. Powdered to a healthy sheen, their wrinkled fingers wrapped around dark walking sticks of elaborate beauty suggested the indulgences collected from pilgrims of the faith seeking to buy a path to heaven left its mark of prosperity on the clergy. Added to the abundance displayed, many of these clerics sported expensive, stunning robes made of red and white silks, imported by the trade established through Hanseatic merchants.

Among them all, one man stood out, a spindly yet boorish-looking man, appearing incongruous in his silks and the heavy golden chain that drooped down his shoulders. A bishop's hat sat on his head, and as he looked at the building in progress, a muscle in his face shuddered against his jutting jaw. The Chain halted his band of men and, turning back, approached the group of debating nobles of the church. As he did so, the Archbishop, breaking off from the discussion, turned to look at the Chain with dark, almost foreboding, black eyes while the subordinates around him continued to debate the construction.

"Be this some cursed Visigothic custom? Nay, it be downright absurd! Any respectable chapel or church in this Most-Holy empire should have nay part in such a preposterously sharp arch…"

"But if ye can't see that, ye must either be addled or blind! The shape is half the beauty. In truth, I reckon…"

At the Chain's approach two well-armored guards appointed on either side of the bishop went to meet the Chain's company. After a moment's inquiry and taking a position of security, the guards escorted only Petres the remainder of the distance approaching the holy man.

"Otto, my friend," The Chain drawled, his grin as unnatural and unnerving as ever. "I brought ye more fodder."

The sudden sound of Petres address to the Archbishop brought a gasp from many of the clergy, while others audibly hissed with whispers simpering their concern with the presence of this pack of ruffians.

"Ye… Ye dare not speak to his Holiness in such a manner!" an indignant clergyman with a receding hairline retorted sternly. "Ye be addressing the Archbishop of Magdeburg, ye impertinent—"

"Silence," the Archbishop commanded in slow, measured tone, holding up one ringed hand. Turning to address the Chain, he said, "This matter could have been postponed, Petres."

"I be here fer my coin, yer Holiness," the Chain sneered with malice. "I've no taste for dawdling, so have one of yer lackies fetch it."

Sighing, the Archbishop nodded to one of the men standing to the side and dressed more plainly in brown sackcloth, who scurried away. Striding past the Chain, the Archbishop glanced at each recruit in turn. Yakov's throat suddenly felt very dry as the man's searching gaze settled on him, even if only for a moment. With a dissatisfied grunt, the Archbishop again turned back to the Chain.

"And this be all of them?" he asked.

"Not at all. I've more of them camped outside the city," the Chain replied giving a vague nod toward the river. "Depends on if ye want all. Our search found several would be warriors fer the work of the church."

"I do," the Archbishop said with finality.

The Chain leaned closer to the Archbishop, so the clergy standing in the distance was out of earshot. "I sense something big being planned. Mayhaps?"

The Archbishop, looking over his shoulder responded, "Lately, the Principality of Wolfenbuttel has weighed heavily upon my thought," the Archbishop stated, a furrow creasing his brow. "I've beseeched the Lord for guidance in these matters. Yet foreseeing the actions of the Duke of Brunswick-Luneburg demands careful contemplation and gathering of information. God, alas, does not always provide answers as swiftly as we desire. And thus, at times, we must take action to hasten the course." Peering at the recruited lads down the lane where the Chain left them to wait, the Archbishop's frown deepened.

"And do I detect my men and I have a role to play in all this, am I right?" the Chain inquired with a hushed, malevolent tone.

Returning his attention to Petres he confided, "Indeed, considering the Duke's enigmatic nature, I hold that while the Lord watches over us, steel be also a worthy protector," the archbishop expressed, his tone measured. "Aye, even with our precautions," he added, pausing briefly. "I may find it necessary to call upon thy service in the days to come should Duke Magnus not heed the wisdom of my designs."

"Shall we then haggle over a price…?" The Chain's eyes sparkled with malevolence. "Or mayhaps nay at this moment," he mused, pausing for effect," …fer a man should never rush into such matters," he said, turning back to the Archbishop, his expression suddenly alert with a sinister idea. "However, I dare say I could be of service right away."

"How?" The Archbishop asked.

"I'd lead my fierce comrades," the Chain hissed, his voice akin to serpent's, drawing nearer, "and we'd torment yer foes. Their flesh, we'd affix to their own abodes. Their storehouses, we'd ignite; their caravans we'd raid; their treasures we'd plunder. We'd embrace the role of ruthless marauders," he continued, turning away from the priest, his words dripping with malice. "And, of course, his Holiness could denounce me openly… but yer adversary would wither. If yer gold be mine, let yer wish be my command," he abruptly halted, pivoting to face the Archbishop, and with a grotesque flourish, he kissed the Archbishop's hand, much like a frail woman in a chapel, sealing his nefarious intent.

Pulling his ringed hand back, the Archbishop looked at the Chain with incredulity, the muscle in his jaw still spasming. Regaining decorum, the priest returned, "Ye speak too freely and too much, Petres."

The knight known as Petres the Chain drew himself back to his full height, his grin like a snarling hound, the lines of his face feral and mad. His short red hair, now plastered to his skull, where perspiration ran in rivulets down his leathery face even though the room remained cold, he composed himself once more.

"My apologies, your Holiness," he begged, his eyes gleaming. "I sometimes lose myself, fer I am born fer war!"

Behind the Archbishop, even the priests, who heard little of the exchange, stood startled by the insane intensity of the Chain's face. Several of them crossed themselves or simply looked away. The Archbishop himself, however, grunted in a low voice and looked at the Chain's recruits. Yakov felt himself quail again.

"We should discuss this in private," the Archbishop told Petres in a low tone. The Chain responded by turning to look at the recruits as well. A sly grin slowly turned up the corners of his mouth, his mustache twitching with delight. An unmasked smirk of triumph flashed in his eyes and then vanished with satisfaction.

To his men, Petres exclaimed, "The next encounter we share, ye'll either be warriors or corpses," he promised maliciously, and then the Archbishop nodded to an armed retainer to escort the Chain and the priest away.

Yakov and his peers led by one guard, returned to the mercenary camp. Regrouping with Mikkel and the others, news was meted out. All the recruits, almost fifty strong, accepted sullenly the enrollment of their enlistment to fight in the forces of the Archbishop.

"Y'know," Mikkel started with uncertainty, "do ye reckon it could be somewhat less dreadful than servin' in them other armies or squabblin' with the highborns? He be… well, ain't he a servant of the Almighty? Me mum used to say them priests, they be the God-fearin' sort… that…" He grew quiet as he looked at Yakov shaking his head slowly.

"He be nay a good man," Yakov, locking his gaze to Mikkel's, continued, "He seeks the Chain's help. What good protector of the faith would want to line akin to Petres?"

The half-moon shaped camp darkened as a violet sunset crashed upon them. They spent the night in restless silence. Petres the Chain did not reappear at camp that night. Some of the mercenaries grumbled, though with humor, that their fearless leader shared the warmth of the Church while they shivered by the weak campfires, kept low by a necessary regulation outside city walls.

"He be chasin' nuns, I tell ye," Yakov heard a voice say as he tried to meander off into sleep.

"Oo, you filthy knave," another voice replied with a hoarse chuckle. "Maybe I'll tell 'im ye said that."

"He'll love it, mark me words, man—but no, 'tis truth. He says he loves them churches more than brothels, even."

"Oh? I ne'er thought 'im t'be that proper."

Another chuckle followed. "Aye, that's the truth, fer he ain't the holy type. But on one wretched day in the middle of some campaign, there he stood, soaked to the bone with blood on his pants, and he says to us, 'I fancy the brothels, lads, but the chapels are closer to me heart!' We stared, thinking he'd gone daft or turned soft. So, we ask and he replied, 'You go to one to lose your coin, and to the other to earn it. Fer I'd rather have gold in me purse than blood on me britches!'"

The voices laughed, and Yakov looked ahead with cool, dispassionate eyes, knowing he would not sleep this night. Nearby, Mikkel tossed and turned in his sleep; Yakov contented himself by listening to his snorting breath.

Then at the rendering of dawn, before the Chain returned, a man from Magdeburg appeared to escort them into the city's barracks. "Up, up!" came his businesslike voice, forcing them into a queue, bleary-eyed and reluctant. As they packed and filed out through the camp with their sparse, looted arms, carrying slings of meager supplies on their backs, Yakov studied the faces of the mercenaries— rough and scarred, sun-toughened and bearded, callous yet obscene. For a moment, he tried to picture himself as a man of the sword among men of the sword.

Then he remembered he barely knew how he looked nowadays to begin with—and with a chuckle at the absurdity of it all, resigning to accept whatever lay before him, followed the rest of the Archbishop's army into the future.

***

"Yakov? You awake?"

Time passed, though Yakov lost count of the hours. The mornings and evenings and nights collapsed into a series of callouses, scars, sores, and bruises. Training an army preparing for eventual war worsened daily through the regimen of the Chain's tough belief in readiness. The drills came every day, sometimes twice a day. The beatings for insubordination happened far too often, and any reprieve for the drudgery imbued few and far between. Even Sundays, after Church, marches, often long and grueling, brought little rest for tired bodies.

"Yakov?" the whisper repeated.

The food, at least, marked improvement from the camp, being construed as more favorable than stale bread, once or twice even included spices, and came willingly donated by a member of the clergy trying to bolster his reputation for generosity. There was, however, a paucity of alcohol; for, like the others, occasionally, drink found its way to Yakov's lips. He remained suspicious of liquor, and the image of his drunk uncle stumbling through his house would never leave him; nonetheless, even Yakov admitted the joy of good, warm beer on a cold night…

"Yakov!" came a hiss.

Sighing, Yakov opened his eyes from the half-dream floating in his mind, turned around in the hay-covered cot he called a bed and peered at the bunk next to his where Mikkel reclined. Around them, two dozen such cots cramped into a small space constituted one of the many buildings in the barracks in Magdeburg.

"Wha… what?" Yakov hissed back, trying to keep his voice low and mask his annoyance at being awakened.

"I jus' need someone to… to hear this," Mikkel then fell quiet. Yakov waited, curious but silent as well. In the dimness of the barracks, he caught a glimpse of Mikkel's tear-streaked cheek. *Am I seein' things,* he wondered, *Or be he weepin'?*

"Yakov, I can't remember me mum's face anymore," Mikkel said, his whispering voice scared. "I used to remember how she died—I still remember seein' the horse and bandit chasing her, but her face… I can't remember… Yakov."

At a loss, Yakov felt a catch in his throat as he thought of his own mother, sitting listlessly in a bed, slits of moonlight falling against her emotionless features. In the fog of his own thought a strange notion came to him, *maybe I imagined it all? Mayhaps she nay really be dead—me own mother?* he wondered and feared the loss of his own remembrance.

Then shaking the web of drifting thought form his mind, pausing, he said, "Mayhaps…" rational thought slowly returned. "…Ye forgot fer a reason," he said trying to encourage Mikkel. "Mayhaps we needs to ferget sometimes t'live."

There was no answer, though Yakov then heard his friend sniffle in the dark. Eyes open, Yakov looked up at the low ceiling, no longer content to sleep, at least if his friend was suffering. Nothing could be said, nothing to make Mikkel feel better, no magical joke or advice to still his sob-wracked silhouette in the next cot.

Many nights spent in their new lodgings would follow, yet together, one crying for a lost past and one remembering a home left behind, passed just this night, quietly providing solace each to the other.

Chapter XI: Soldiers

"What a distinction it is to fight for something, and what foolishness it is to fight for something you don't believe in!"

-Unknown Monk, circa 1381

Yakov sharpened the head of his spear, his face firm and wooden as nearby cold water sprayed from a fountain in the town square. Sitting uneasily on a wooden bench near the spray of water, he stroked the spearhead with a whetstone. The feeling of the closeness of the bleached white walls of Schoningen crushed in upon his senses. The plain town, now bright white in the light of a heatless sun, gave Yakov an intense wariness of what lurked around him. A church bell tolled somewhere. He tried to ignore the sound, the foreboding feeling intruding on his alertness. Added to this, curious heads of children peered from the windows of the very buildings which held his attention.

The hard years did not pass quickly for the young man who became a soldier. Now near two heads taller, though his face still pale, and the rosiness of his cheeks replaced with a gaunt look, Yakov, lips set in a firm line always his, looked every bit the warrior ready to accept any confrontation. His hair, now cropped short on the sides and the back, fell over his forehead greasily in a typical soldier's haircut. Dark circles under his eyes marked a testament to the sleepless nights spent on quick marches. A chainmail coif lay uncoiled around his neck, and he wore a thick red and white gambeson. Dark trousers covered his legs. Though his shoulders appeared wider, grown spindly, his frame set to his task, the long lance across his lap. His long legs seemed uncomfortable as he bent toward the fountain, wetting the spearhead before continuing to hone a sharp tip to his weapon.

"They're bringing the rear in now," came a voice. Yakov turned to see Mikkel striding up to him. Years changed boys to men, and so Mikkel grew. His face, now pockmarked from a bout of vicious acne, coupled with his scruffy beard, made him look older than his age. Taller now, though not but half Yakov's growth, he wore a simple gambeson and coif, plus thick, quilted gloves, topped off with a rag tied around his head. Now imbued with a new confidence, he stopped and stood stalwart, his spear relaxed against the curve of his neck, and peered at Yakov through vigilant eyes, a slight grin curling the corners of his mouth.

Yakov grunted. "They saying why w're here?"

"Aye, probably just to let someone or the other know we're here," Mikkel said, shrugging. "Our leader says tis 'deterrence.' "

"What deterrence?" Yakov scoffed, looking back at his spear cynically. "If someone wants the town so bad, they'll attack."

Mikkel sighed. "The Archbishop just won this town two months ago, man. He can't leave this place undefended, now, can he?"

Yakov grunted again. Only a few days ago, he entered the town and watched as the dead were still being removed. Though most who died only starved in the siege and not through any combat--no, that was not true, he decided. The desire to control killed them...stubborn attitudes killed them as dead as any arrow or spear could accomplish. Yakov and Mikkel arrived alongside the advance party to help prepare the town for the arrival of the Archbishop. Corpses needed to be dragged out of cramped little houses to clean the city for the arrival, and it fell to Yakov, Mikkel and the other recruits to accomplish this as quickly as possible.

As the Archbishop arrived, a scuffle occurred. Some men, furious at the siege, gathered to protest at the entourage. Yakov remembered the sinking feeling when their commander, Niklas the Quick, received an order to dispel the protestors immediately. All Yakov remembered from the blur of events to follow was stepping behind a tree to puke, his spear covered in blood. Now, as he leaned his back against the tree, he remembered a thought from years ago on a night in the barracks.

Maybe humans need to ferget sometimes t'live.

Retuning his stare to the bloodied spear tip once more, he purged himself yet again with the realization his spear found a mark somewhere in the chaos. *Nay return existed in the mind of a door once opened,* Yakov thought. In the flash of time, his life had changed dramatically in a new direction.

***

The thoughts of the past couple of days haunted Yakov, but he was able to return to the business of being a soldier, now working again to sharpen his spear. He slowly ran his whetstone over its edges and contemplated his life. His attitude towards his soldier's life now changed; he surmised himself no longer the youngster he was only a week ago. He spent quite a bit of down time thinking about his own moral bearing. Not many friends could be found like Mikkel, but Mikkel still made quick and often rash decisions with consequences that often landed him in trouble with his higher ups. Yakov did not relish this way of life any longer. He found more comfort in thinking about home and his sister and brother and how he might return some day.

"The spear be keen enough, ain't it," Mikkel said carefully.

Yakov, startled from his reverie, sighed, knowing he was still being careful around Mikkel. "Did ye really need to creep up on me like that?" Yakov exclaimed.

Leaning the spear against a rough wall with weeds growing on it, near the fountain, Yakov got up, stretching. He saw the dark silhouettes of children darting away from the windows to hide. Mikkel must have as well as they both laughed.

"Like as not, they be dreamin' 'bout wieldin' swords and spears themselves," Mikkel chuckled.

"I reckon so," Yakov replied, glancing backward. "Swords and spears. What's the big fuss 'bout 'em anyhow?"

"Ain't much," Mikkel conceded, scanning their surroundings. "But we ought nay be dawdlin' here. Niklas don't want us minglin' too much with the folks. If them less-than-cheerful locals get hold of one of us, it could lead to more bloodshed. Catchin' my drift?"

Yakov looked at Mikkel and then simply nodded a knowing nod. *So now he be worried 'bout getting' in trouble,* Yakov thought.

The two friends walked back to the barracks. Despite being a town, Schöningen was not particularly large. The quaint architecture was simplistic, clearly not designed with aesthetics in mind. The pale buildings were topped with plain shingles and dull tiles, and the trapped rainwater between raised cobbles tinted the earth a mossy green. Yakov looked at the empty chicken-houses; clearly there was no meat to spare in the town. Deepening the existing shallow mine entered the local talk with some excitement, but no one initiated the work. Even though some supplies entered the town earlier after the initial rationing of relief food, people simply could not afford more supplies from the merchants. The merchants would want to hold collateral any land or holdings for advancement of funds, and too much distrust existed between the common folk and the merchants. The Archbishop promised talks would be held with the merchants to free the food supply, but, again, no such talks materialized.

The barracks in the town were a collection of squat buildings with the colors of the Archbishop raised from the flags and banners. Crooked trees stood stiffly across the open, grassy yards, and half-dressed soldiers sat lazily under the sun, trying to soak in as much of the weak sunlight with their naked backs as possible.

As they passed under the perfectly curved, graceful arch of the gate, Yakov wondered, *How must it feel to make something akin to that? To create instead of destroy, to put yer strength and will into making something as simple, yet solid and worthy as that arch.* And yet, just as quickly, his contemplation, formed by his now world, changed. Sarcasm sneaked in and around the corners of innocent thoughts. *Whoever made it, made it only for the sake of a living.*

Mayhaps no expression of the creator could be found in it at all—mayhaps, on a second thought, *nay different than him swinging his spear around.* In the vague memories of his father, Yakov still remembered him sitting outside in the open on a tree stump, whittling away at wood with the experienced, scarred hands of a craftsman, hoping to add some extra clink to the family purse by the end of each month, which could, if lucky, translate to new, warmer clothes by the end of the year.

Yakov scowled at the fool's errand his father embraced in that distant past. His departure left Yakov's mother and older sister, younger brother, and himself to fend for themselves. Hans, Yakov's father, left Uncle Karl, his father's brother—an uncle prone to drink away any income the family could muster—to care for the family and work the farm.

Thoughts of home left Yakov with the emotional burden of distance, as well as a want to return. Months, maybe years, he could not remember exactly, had slipped by in a fog of reality. Yakov's promise lay fresh in his mind even though distance and time filtered its urgency. Going home to find his loved ones, with the means to help the family farm regain its worth, welded a vague awareness to his soul.

Yakov scowled darkly and shook his head, as if trying to dislodge a stubborn thought as the soldiers walked across the courtyard. Fallen leaves fluttered in the breeze as they passed, and Yakov looked up distractedly as a squat, wall of a man rolled into his field of vision. He was not particularly tall, but he was wide. More than anyone else, he wore a haubergeon, the short-sleeved, abbreviated chain mail shirt then covered by a breastplate and tabard. Under one arm he carried his visorless helm. A prodigious moustache hung low over his sparse beard, a darker brown than his hair, which were pulled back to reveal a receding hairline. Serious, but not unkind, grey eyes flitted from man to man under a heavy brow. His fingers drummed calmly over the hilt of his sheathed sword. From its hilt hung a weapon which reflected in a way too polished for the likes of the scarred and ruddy-faced warrior now standing before the company.

"Niklas the Quick," Mikkel nodded, and their leader nodded back seriously. Next to Niklas stood a bald, dour man addressed as Franz. His role soon became obvious as Niklas's secretary and herald. Franz's responsibilities were given to the reading and writing appropriate for the position and occasion. Yakov looked at Mikkel, who returned a smirk; both agreed in silent acknowledgment that Franz created a layer of pomp where the politics of the occasion needed to establish a clear pecking order in the ranks.

"The townsfolk seem a mite restless," Franz reported, assuming an air of great significance as he cleared his throat. "In a certain instance, one of our comrades received a good pelting with a handful of spoiled fruit-merchandise, though whether that qualifies as an assault or not... "

"Aye. For now, tis fruit," said Niklas, abruptly interrupting Franz, frowning impressively, now casting authority, "And on the morrow it shall be stones." He paused and scowled, whereupon Franz withdrew. "Several of our scouts have relayed accounts of isolated occurrences, individually insignificant mayhaps, but collectively indicative of a deeper concern, one that could prove perilous. Animosity, it appears, does not easily dissipate. Indeed, it may linger indefinitely. The populace has grown to harbor a deep-seated aversion towards us—and in light of our actions, God forgive us, I..." He trailed off, then suddenly looked at Yakov and Mikkel again, as though only seeing them properly now. "Ye there, both of ye—what have your observations revealed within the town? Must I anticipate waking up on the morrow with a pitchfork lodged in my breastplate?"

Yakov eyed his leader apprehensively and then responded, "Everything appears ordinary and normal, Sire." Yakov said plainly.

Mikkel shot a quick look at him before chiming in, "The roads looked somewhat abandoned, and I got the sense folks were steerin' clear of us. Not a lot," he rushed to add, "but it be noticeable." Yakov looked back at Mikkel with a pinched expression. Mikkel just gave a satisfied glance in return.

Niklas, now asserting command, continued to frown. "Better than outright rebellion, mayhaps, but it remains a troubling sign. If they shun our presence, who can say what clandestine discussions they engage in? Franz, what tidings do our soldiers gather from the taverns and alehouses?"

Franz, shifting from his spot between Yakov and Mikkel to stand before them, took his place beside Niklas, and paused. "Well, this here's naught but a bit of hearsay, so I'm a tad unsure 'bout bringin' it up…"

"Spit it out, man," Niklas sighed, tapping at the hilt of his sword with fresh impatience.

"Word's goin' 'round 'bout some sort of liberator, or so they say," he cautiously mentioned.

Niklas looked at his secretary with alarm. "What? A force of men? Where from?"

"Nay, sire. It be more akin to…" Franz hesitated, a touch embarrassed. "It be more like a tale, sire. Like one o' them destined heroes from the stories, sire. The folks, they dub him 'the fletcher.' Der Flechtemann—a mere legend, nothin' else. I reckon there ain't a man like that in the real world, sire."

Yakov and Mikkel could only smile inwardly as the good secretary Franz attempted to quell the anxiety of his sire. The two knew all too well that the myth of der

Flechtemann carried with it more than something that simply paralleled tales of witches and goblins.

"Legends have a way o' bitin' back," Niklas remarked with a cautious, furrowed brow. "Tales give men hope, and a man with hope can accomplish great deeds. I've witnessed it… men can rush headlong into spears, they can tread on hot coals, they can subsist on nothin' but moss for days when they cling to their faith. We must be ready. This fervor must not be permitted to establish itself."

"But sir…" Franz said weakly.

"No!" the knight barked, wiping sweat from his forehead as he suddenly marched to the middle of the square. "Men! *Gather here!*" he bellowed. In ones and twos men emerged from the buildings or reluctantly dragged themselves away from the sun pulling the shirts on and boots up.

"Soldiers,, you be well aware of the saccifices we've made to secure this village, these fields. You understand the deeds we've undertaken to safeguard it!" he exclaimed, looking at each man in turn with a tough, unblinking stare. Yakov felt his stomach sink yet again as he remembered the blood on his spear; some of the other soldiers looked down, as though clearly trying not to think back, while others looked unbothered, even bored.

"This be what we do," the Niklas continued. "Our duty be to the Archbishop and the church. The Archbishop is a man of God who intercesses for us. For it be only through the sanctity of the priesthood we can find salvation. We cannot approach the altar of Heaven without the indulgences of the clergy. Whatever ill will the men of this town hold toward us, we cannot allow it to hold us back. The order of society depends on our ability to interpret the will of the Church. For it be only through the Archbishop and the clergy of the Church that we truly know the will of God. We be not here to be loved. We be not here to be ignored. But aye, we be here to enforce the true nature of order in the name of the Archbishop—and we must maintain the decorum of the Church, nay the cost.”

A general nervous mumble of uneasiness moved through the gathered troops. Some of the men, Yakov noted, shifted their stance from foot to foot or yawned in the midday sun, itching to return to their leisure, as uncaring about the speech as they were about the slaughter of the last few days.

“Idle tales and supposed champions,” Niklas uttered as he extended his harangue. “Foolish chatter flourishes here about this…der Flechtemann…etch the name into your memory, let it sear into yer minds.” Niklas pressed on, an air of self-importance creeping into his voice. Gazing into the eyes of his assembled troops, he declared, “If any soul, be it man or woman, dares to utter that name in this town, ye shall accuse them of sedition.”

He continued—his fists clenched at his side. The sound of his raised voice now echoing from the buildings around the town square. “Any hushed conversation in a tavern, any marketplace whisper about heroes here to save them—do the same. Fill the dungeons if needed, if only fer a week or so. Remember,” he yelled hoarsely, “if they be allowed to gather hope in their ranks, they will rebel—and if they rebel, they will die. This be… it be the only way to bring salvation for them and restore peace to the countryside 'round." Their commander took a long pause and steadied his voice, "So, get prepared. From today forward, I don't want to see any of ye lounging about with nothing to do. We be at war with this absurd myth of theirs… and it be the myth we dispel with our actions today!" Silence cast its spell over the assembled. And then, more attentive, the men dispersed. Some half-hearted cheers arose, and others began to mumble uneasily.

The echo of the Archbishop's silent directive to him now committed to his men, he stood down from his perch beside the fountain. Concern ransacked his face. As their leader turned to leave, Yakov saw sweat dripping from his face.

He be afraid, Yakov realized. Even from a distance, he knew his knight well enough to know he was not willfully cruel. After what must have been the Archbishop's harsh order, Niklas the Quick tried to find an alternate way to deal with the foreboding atmosphere in the small town, but the will of the Archbishop forced his absolute verdict. There would be no room for interpretation. Now, watching the broad shoulders of the Niklas the Quick retreat, he noticed the stiffness of his commander's back, the sweat running in desperate rivulets down his neck.

The same goosey shiver swam down the back of Yakov's own neck, a cautious notion signaling possible events to come.

***

That night, Yakov awoke to some caterwaul or cry outside the walls of the assigned bivouac. The fog of sleep slowly found its way from his eyes as awareness made its way to reality. Mikkel, sleeping next to him, abruptly snorted awake with a confused start, his countenance a deathly pale in the moonlight. Exchanging a panicked glance, the two hurried outside along with the rest of the men, who slowly became aware of the commotion. Grabbing cudgels from a weapon-rack next to the doorway put there for emergencies just such as this, they appeared one by one from the darkened quarters. As each man emerged into the dark of the early morning, they formed a crowd of soldiers assembled into a confused, chaotic throng swarming into the courtyard. In the mass of uncertainty, Mikkel held onto Yakov's shoulders and jumped up once to catch a quick glance of whatever was happening.

"What is the problem?" Yakov asked impatiently.

"A trespasser," Mikkel said with a mix of excitement and dread in his voice. "The night guard caught someone in the courtyard!"

"*Who sent ye?*" came the harsh roar of Niklas.

Yakov winced. A hush fell over the mob of confused soldiers as they made their way forward. A view of the courtyard opened to Yakov and Mikkel as many others began to step apart to their pressing. The view now before them unveiled an odd sight in the mirky darkness. In the quiet of the assembled a breeze blew silently, leaves fluttered along the ground in the night air, and a dog barked in the distance.

Yakov heard an odd, mewling sound coming from what appeared to be a man crumpled on the cobbles, wracking with sobs. In the half-dark moonlight, huddled a shabby and ill-sewn tunic draped around visage of a person. If not for the shivering of lumpy sackcloth and the sound of mewling which came from the form on the ground, a sack for potatoes would have been more descriptive. The man's face to the ground in quaking obeisance, and shaggy, dark hair bloomed on the stone courtyard like a pool of blood puddling around the captive's head as he degraded himself before the regimental leader.

With a foot over the man's back stood Niklas, his usually mild eyes wide as he breathed hard. Franz, the assertive attendant, stood at a distance, watchful eyes darkly accusing as his sire drew his sword. Yakov thought he noticed the gleaming sword shake for a moment in the moonlight.

"Who?" he demanded again, now kicking the man in the side. The figure turned over, revealing the scrunched, sobbing face of a remarkably unsightly man with a bloody nose, his pockmarked visage riddled with sores and blisters.

"No 'un," the man yelped, tears freely streaming down his rippling cheeks. Niklas bared his teeth in a gesture that seemed more desperate than fierce to Yakov, placing the point of the sword to the man's neck.

"Ye came with a tinderbox and made for the stables yonder...ye made for *the hay*," the commander snarled...though his eyes locked to his prisoner's. "You would have *burned us in our sleep!*" Niklas moved the sword tip under the man's chin and forced the derelict to rise to his knees. "Who sent ye? Be it... be it that damn der Flechtemann?"

There was a sudden hush as the man abruptly paused his mewling. He blinked, and then. as Yakov watched incredulously, a strange, mad smile stretched on the man's face.

"'E didn't send me," he said with a gap-toothed grin. His chest shuddered as though still sobbing. "But e'll come for you... 'un day. Y'killed 'em all! *Killed...* 'em all. Dog. You's a rich man's *dog!*"

Deadly quiet fell on the clearing as the man's chest heaved with effort, his face caught between a smile and a sob.

From the crowd of men, another figure entered the clearing. Yakov recognized him from a previous meeting as knight of one of the other two companies stationed alongside them. Long-beard, the Long-beard of Hasse, now approached stroking the venerable namesake. As he neared, he acknowledged Niklas with an unrecognizable grunt and roughly pushed the captive back to the ground. Raising his booted foot quickly, he kicked the grinning man in the face once.

"Ye insolent fool! Can ye not see a servant of the Archbishop standin' here?" admonished Long-beard.

The figure shrieked. A tooth slowly dropped to the cobbles held by a thread of syrupy blood. "E'll come for you… 'un day…he will…der Flechtemann will," the cowed man repeated, now rolling onto his back on the courtyard.

"This bloke appears to have lost his marbles, Niklas. Allow me to settle him," Long-beard said, grabbing the hilt of his own sword. He stared at the prone, bleeding man with a mixture of pity and revulsion. Niklas clenched his jaw in anger and glared at Long-beard, who raised his eyebrows in trepidation as he stepped back, not willing to cross the anger of Niklas.

A sudden composure fell on Niklas the Quick's face.

As the man on his back looked up in pained horror, the commander's gleaming sword, the tip now purchased back to the prisoner, sunk into his throat. A piteous, ugly whine came from the man as his eyes teared up again. After three slow, gurgling breaths, there was silence.

As the men whispered and dispersed, Yakov and Mikkel stood with their cudgels held in clammy hands, their minds agape at the sight just passed. They watched, too, as Long-beard of Hasse approached and clapped the still, silent Niklas on the back, whispering some quiet encouragement of camarederie to him.

Perhaps it was only Yakov who saw and recognized the look in Niklas the Quick's eyes—the same empty, dark look once seen in the eyes of a young boy named Hanno.

Chapter XII: Rebels

"How easily Kings fear the word 'rebellion'! O, but how rarely they ask why men rebel…"

-Unknown Monk, circa 1383

It was dawn when the first rebel scout reached the outskirts of Schoningen.

His name, though not called such in some time, was Elias. For the most part, he had spent the last year in near silence, drifting from village to village in the disguise of an itinerant hunter, gathering information and picking up hidden supplies left behind by sympathizers in unlikely places. Even now, as he dismounted from his pallid grey horse, he, first and foremost, needed to sense the climate of the town. What word was spoken in the streets about the resistance movement? His desire to seek out friends of the movement, the more subversive elements, directed his cloaked information gathering.

Within sight of the town, though still far enough away, it appeared a jumble of pale buildings under the pink sky. Guiding his horse to a nearby coppock of trees, the only copse for some distance, he carefully checked the bark of each tree—and there he spied the sign for which he looked, a single, curving tree with the makeshift shape of an arrow crudely hacked into it by a hand-ax.

Elias touched the bark and nodded. He felt moved by a great, overpowering emotion; this carving meant the folk within the walls knew of the great Der Flechtemann. Using a practical code invented by the man himself, Elias knew, perhaps better than most, to the people inside the town, this announced a prayer of hope. When barons and Archbishops, the dispensers of divine providence, arrived to besiege towns and seize stored viands, all that was left were starved subjects. Only fabled stories could help assuage the comparable cruelty of Caesars warned against in old texts. Myths passed from person to person by crafty scouts, lookouts, or bards often brought joy and entertainment to the young sitting by the hearth, though wiser minds understood the warnings or assurances of each story received.

Especially true stories.

Now, turning away from the tree, Elias made his way back to his horse. It would be easy enough, he surmised, to move into the town. All he would need is to first get word back to the great Fletcher himself before donning his usual itinerant's ragged cloak. He was sure now he would quickly find friends among the people. He would make his usual rounds of the taverns, the drinking houses, the old courtyards where men talk in hushed voices. Too, he would search the wells, whereby the wary women would exchange gossip; also, those hidden alcove-houses where conspirators would gather each week to speak ill of kings before dissipating into routines of forced normalcy.

With a small, determined smile, Elias knew the work ahead would be difficult—but with the smirk on his face, he eagerly welcomed the task charged to him.

***

Anna watched Sieghart as he rode before her, his hair grown longer, shimmering in the crimson noon-sun as they made their way under the dappled shadows of old, sleeping trees. At the head of the column of the rebels, he led the party through a winding mud-path, sitting at-ease in the saddle of his unruly bay as his loose shoulders jostled in rhythm to the horse's canter. She herself rode a sparse, roan horse, barely more than a pony. Beside and behind her, four shabby caravans shuddered along the muddy path, carrying the rebels' equipment and the camp supplies.

Der Flechtemann's cipher, just a few months before, scrawled across a crumpled parchment, brought with it the intended command for the next rebel movement. Anna only caught a glimpse of scribbles and scratches on the torn bit of cloth, and even though she could not read, she became aware of its importance to the band of rebels. Upon its arrival, Sieghart called the band together and read the note aloud before the camp.

Break camp and head for Schoningen. Form listenin' posts along the outskirts. Ye will have friends there. Will join ye by the comin' of Autumn.

And so Sieghart slipped almost immediately back into his role as leader-in-absentia. Anna knew him for long enough and now observed, acutely aware of how much all the others looked up to him—and why. He was always supportive when needed, never afraid to join in the chores or to help the women with the everyday scrubbing of the pans. Expecting nothing in return, he helped chop wood for the fire with the easy confidence of a man, the leader he could be expected to be. Sieghart loved their company genuinely; this much was obvious to anyone. Sitting by the campfires at night, his bright observant eyes reflected the firelight as he marveled at the faces around him, his expression tempered by a contended smile.

Anna felt her face grow warm as she blushed. More and more over time, she found herself stealing glances at him. Even now, she caught herself sneaking another quick look as he half-turned, unaware of her attention, to look at a rabbit scampering past. In that quick moment. she noticed the fuzzy stubble of a beard beginning to appear against his jaw. Now recentering his attention, out of the corner of his eye, Sieg caught Anna's glance; he returned a requited smile, and waved her over to ride alongside him. Drawn into sudden awareness of Sieg's gaze, Anna, warmed by the intimacy, smiled inwardly; for his bright eyes showed no loss of their boyish spark. Her blush now more aflame, she complied.

"Are ye well?" he asked with a frown as her horse cantered up to keep pace with him. "Ye look feverish."

"I'm fine," Anna said, eager to change the subject. "Why be we going to…?" She trailed off, trying to remember the town's name.

"Schoningen," Sieg said, looking ahead with a thoughtful air. "It be a small enough town, recently taken by a churchman for a prize—there be war in those parts in these days. I don't entirely understand our leader's strategy for taking us there, but—" He shrugged. "He be never wrong b'fore."

Anna nodded as they continued for a while in pleasant silence. After a bit of time passed, a breeze whispered at her cheek, bringing with it the feeling of being watched. Anna turned around to see her brother staring at her sardonically as he perched beside the caravan driver in the wagon following them.

Dieter, now grown, albeit much faster than expected, at least than Anna expected, looked back at her. With his big eyes and ruddy, freckled cheeks, she thought she glimpsed Yakov in him, his older brother. Years passed by quickly, too quickly, yet she could still see Yakov in her mind's eye. Earning enough to pay the farm debts left by their uncle Karl had sent Yakov off to some unknown existence. If not for the middle-parted hair and the bright green of his eyes, Dieter might have been his twin. A lump formed in her throat at the thought of Yakov, but she pushed it away—and in any case, Dieter's shoulders were wider than what she remembered of Yakov. Dieter, growing up in a camp with adequate food and plenty of chores, had grown into a frame broad for his age. He now stared intently at Anna, and she could not help but notice his vexed expression.

Jus' get on with it, his face seemed to say. Flushed, she returned his scowl. This new agitation of his toward her began to annoy her. *What question came between them now,* she frowned, taking her attention away from Dieter. *Get on with what?* Came the confused muddle of her mind.

"I be keeping ye from your brother," said Sieghart, who was looking at her closely. He glanced back just in time to catch Dieter's vigilant eye. "Y'should ride with him."

"Nay, he'll be fine," Anna said, stiffly straightening in the saddle. Changing the subject she added, "He jus' hoped to ride a horse today."

Sieghart, a bit unassured, laughed. "Well, that would explain it. I bothered me old man to ride to nay end when I be yer brother's age."

Sieg's father was never mentioned in their conversations before, and, for a moment, Anna wondered whether she should ask about him. Glancing a look at him. she noticed the faraway look in Sieg's eyes, the disappointed curl of his lip, and realized it was not a question she should ask now.

They rode on in silence. Just as the sun began to dip below the distant mountains, their scout returned with news of a camp area nearby. In the fading indigo afterglow of the new-vanquished sunset, they stumbled after the hunched scout as he led them to a clearing just off the trail where the jutting trees formed a natural ring around a mass of mossy boulders. At first sight, the arrangement of rocks appeared to be a natural formation, but as the group dismounted and began the work of making torches to light the ground, a murmur spread through the band, they may be camped near a giant's cairn.

As Dieter and Anna helped set up the tents with practiced efficiency, Anna noticed Sieghart near the stones, studying them with his hands on his waist.

"Don't yer eyes hurt?" Dieter said to his sister, annoyance in his voice.

"I don't know what ye mean," she shot back, immediately defensive. "And that be nay the way to talk to yer elders. Now, hand me that canvas," she said, still looking in Sieghart's direction. Now distracted by Dieter's rustle of equipment behind her, she turned, "Nay, not that one—the big one."

Soon enough, the camp set around them found others bustling here and there with campfires warming evening meals. Some of the men sat around as well, half-lying down, easing their travel-sores. On Anna's circle of stones and a crackling fire sat a prodigious pot filled with water. As she waited for it to boil, she saw Sieg return, and sitting on the opposite side of the cooking fire, warmed his hands.

"I saw ye by the giant-cairn," came Dieter's abrupt voice. Sieghart started, just noticing him sitting some distance from the fire, leaning against a fallen log. The boy's green eyes pierced through the night.

"I be by the stones, aye," Sieg said, clearing his throat as his glance flickered between Anna and Dieter. "But 'tis nay giant-cairn."

Anna frowned. "Well, it does look like a cairn."

"If it be, 'tis built by men, nay giants," Sieg said, looking at his hands. "Humans can do anythin'. We can build anythin'. We can destroy anythin'. Shape anythin', change anythin'."

"Aye," said one of the rebels, a bony-faced man with a crooked scar. "But humans can't lift nay stones like that. We couldn't lift that ourselves, all of us here in a go."

"We could," came Dieter's thoughtful voice, and Sieghart looked at him curiously. "With ropes."

"Ropes?" the scarred man repeated, amused, but grew quiet as Sieg raised a hand.

"Aye, he's right, with ropes," said Sieghart, his voice alive. "With ropes and sturdy beasts of burden, with leverage and stout staffs, and with plenty of able-bodied folk, 'tis doable. I this day and age, folks raise castles grander than this'un, be they towering and noble or stout and dauntless. What be but a pile of stones in the face of a man's resolve?"

The scarred man thought about it for a moment, and then grinned. "Still seems like giant-work to me."

Sieg shook his head in mock disappointment and a chuckle rose around the fire. Anna smiled to herself as she let the vegetables and dried strips of dark meat drop into the gently frothing water. The night air was calm and cool, and the men around nearby fires began to hum a wordless tune. It was the sort of lilting tune mothers would sing to their children—wordless, but so old and common, that almost every man around the fire knew it. They hummed the music to themselves, and Sieghart looked skyward with a distant smile, half worried about the coming days, half in love with this moment. He caught Anna's glance for a moment, and his smile deepened. Her heart fluttered.

Later, as the broth's color began to emerge, Anna turned to call her brother to eat. Instead, she found him asleep in the distant red fire-glow beside his log. As the others began to eat, she debated whether to wake him, and decided against it. She smiled tiredly and, taking off her thick, woolen shawl, draped it over him, tucking it in despite his sleepy grumbling.

As each portion of broth came and went. Finally, the others began to crawl back into their tents, eager to sleep after a hard day on the road. Only she and Sieghart remained beside the fire, picking at mostly empty bowls of food as they sat beside each other. Hesitating, his hand found hers, careful as though her fingers would steal themselves away at his touch. But her hand stayed where it was, warm under his calloused fingers. They exchanged a look at one another. Anna's face was red, framed by a careless halo of golden hair, burning in the firelight.

The intoxicating magnetism of the moment slowly drew Anna and Sieg together. They kissed, at first lightly touching lips and then deeply experiencing the pent-up emotions of days not knowing the mind of the other. Abruptly, without warning, Anna broke away from their embrace. Sitting back and looking at Sieg, her eyes bright and dazed. "I want this, but… I don't…"

"I'll marry ye," Sieghart blurted. Anna's eyes widened. "I'll do it properly, I…well…"

She looked at his boyishly flustered expression and suddenly broke into laughter. He looked at her, mildly lost as she laughed until her eyes teared up. He had never seen her laugh like this before, and Anna herself did not know whether she had ever laughed so pure a laugh as now her love spilled out for Sieg. Then, feeling a bit foolish, Sieghart began to chuckle as well, and their laughter became music of its own under the stars.

Chapter XIII: Woes of Men

"Men have many woes; how many pains there are! There...is the taxation and the drought, the fallen crop and the plague, the siege and the war, whatever [war] it be...and men rise and fall, but the woes remain."

-Unknown Monk, circa 1384

In the heart of Schoningen, there nestled a drinking-house called Zur Krone—the Crown. With its crown-painted façade marred by neglect, the establishment stood as a resilient bastion, its sturdy timbers weathered by the tides of time and conflict. Two bearded men sat outside of a heavy oak door, surreptitiously looking around as they pretended to play a game of dice. A black-capped man walked past, nodding at them, before entering through the doors. His grey cloak clung to bony shoulders as he walked with guarded steps.

Venturing through the oak portal, the man felt a familiar burst of scents—a heady mélange of aged wines, smoldering embers, and the lingering essence of long-spent incense. Dim light filtered through smudged casements, illuminating the suspended particles of dust. Worn tables, scarred by countless elbows and tankards, bore the weight of burly workmen and drunkards wasting away at their cups, holding onto the wooden tankards with desperate tenacity.

The black-capped man's footsteps barely disturbed the aged floorboards, carrying him with a purposeful grace amidst the sea of revelry. His piercing gaze, concealed beneath the brim of his hat, darted from face to face, searching a trusted visage. Whispers, like tendrils of smoke, trailed in his wake, intertwining with the fervent conversations of the patrons. Words danced upon the air, borne by the clandestine breaths of those discontented with the new, holy ruler's reign. He could feel it in the air—a conspiracy, its tendrils stretching through the shadowed corners of the room where candlelight hesitated to tread.

He approached a dim corner where a group of figures huddled in earnest conference. Their eyes, brimming with shared resolve, met his gaze, conscious of their furtive purpose. He recognized them from his last visit to the city—his original contacts with covert elements of Schoningen.

"Hail, friend," came one low greeting, and removing his black cap, Elias joined their circle. The air grew taut with anticipation.

"What news of—" a man began, only to halt as Elias raised a hand, looking around carefully.

"Peace, friend," Elias warned. He knew der Flechtemann would be the first nervous worry of city authorities. "The walls have ears aplenty. However," pausing again to take in the intent faces around him, "I am sure you were going to mention… *the bard?*"

Tapping the side of his pocked and crooked nose with one scrawny finger and the purvey of a knowing look, with a quick nod, Elias' contact continued. "What news? Be he here yet?"

"He be near, near enough," Elias said coolly, looking around at the expectant faces as he continued to speak in code. *"The company be gatherin' at this very spot. We will have many performers soon,"* he whispered." "And what tidin's from the town?"

"Grim, I'm afraid," one of the men said soberly, forlorn droplets of ale clinging to his forked beard. "Another townsman be put to his grave a few nights back." Peering into his large tankard of the thick ale of the house, ruminating over the memory, "Cäsar sorted hisself a good man. Nay all right in the head, mind ye, but a good man." A long pause enabled the silence in the small group as he took a long swill of his ale, "Lost his mother in the siege, then lost his brothers in the slaughter after it." Simpering wistfully, he continued, "The poor bastard tried to burn the barracks down, …now he lies beside his brothers in the earth."

The men at the table crossed themselves, and Elias followed suite. Looking around to ensure there were no eavesdroppers nearby, Elias bent over the table. "Many a soul, like Casar's, hath met their end in senseless sieges and battles," he murmured, his eyes darting to meet the gazes around the table. "But what do these wars truly serve? Rich men pitted 'gainst rich men, all fer their own gains?"

A dark mutter of assent spread about the table. Their voices, conspiratorial and fervent, wove intrigue. Schemes were thought out, and strategies refined. Eyes around the table glimmered with a hope Elias knew all too well. The same hope remained lit in the depths of his own heart. Those hopes for a world where quiet whisperers would no longer need to conspire in the dark, when there would not be tyrants above tyrants above tyrants, or when the games of the rich and powerful would stop leaving a trail of broken common folk in their wake.

Elias only half listened to their desperate discussion, picking out bits and pieces in the harshness of overlapping accounts where attempts to disrupt the Archbishop and his constabulary, as it were, remained ineffective. So far, resistance efforts at subversion had limited the small band of peers to theft, vandalism, disturbance of the peace, and one failed attempt at arson. *And rightly so*, Elias surmised, *This small group lacked enough teeth to set a mark in this struggle.* In earlier contacts with the underground, Elias, himself, cautioned these well-meaning individuals to stay subtle until the rebels positioned themselves well enough to work quickly and decisively for a greater good. Knowing the movement of forces, nearly complete, allowed his instinct to tell him the time to bite and bite hard, now existed.

"A message must be sent, now," Elias broke in. They looked at him expectantly. "We must arrange for a *performance.* Something to catch the interest of our…holy patrons."

Elias' decisive reaction became clear to the men around the table, who nodded in agreement. "We be forgin' connections with the discontented common folk by the sun's turn, and with each discreet bond, our ranks swell," declared the man adorned with a forked beard. All seated at the table shifted their focus to the conversation unfolding between the two. Silence clung to their clandestine assembly. Elias, scanning each visage around the table, discerned this man to be the ringleader of this covert gathering within the city's confines. The man with the forked beard leaned closer, his eyes brimming with resolve, and spoke, "Reveal yer needs, friend."

"A week from now," Elias said carefully, "The roads to the town, my comrades, might soon turn treacherous, but sustenance shall find its way into the homes of the needy, as if by some divine providence unbeknownst to the heedless," Elias whispered with a hushed tone that held the attention of all seated around the table. "Our loyal compatriots shall commence relieving the merchant convoys joureyin' to and fro the town," he went on, "to maintain the façade, we shall covertly bestow the liberated provisions upon the town's folk."

The man's brow knitted. "But in case of such a...*miracle,* some people will be suspected."

"Aye, this be a favorable course," Elias murmured amongst his fellow partisans in hushed tones. "When the time of reckoning doth arrive," he continued, "Certain brethren from the town shall vanish, their steps marked for all to see. The town's own valiant soldiers shall be hot on their trail."

The man's eyes widened by a fraction. "Ah. But while hunting down such dangerous rebels...well, anythin' could happen to a patrol."

"Anythin' could happen," Elias agreed, and they understood each other. The plan was agreed on. Makeshift maps were made on the table with fingers tracing spilled, sticky ail over the dark wood, only to be wiped clean by a grimy sleeve.

"Gentlemen," Elias finally said, standing up, "'Twill be a performance to remember."

The men at the table nodded. The fork-bearded man smiled. "Me compliments to the bard."

Elias inclined his head. "I'll be leavin' a small gift fer your dear mother. Usual place."

The man nodded again, and slipping the dark felt hat back on his head, Elias gathered his faded grey cloak around him and left. Walking through the town, he clambered easily over a fence, wading through an unkempt herb-garden next to a crumbling stone building. Prying a loose, earthy stone from the wall, Elias withdrew a small pouch from within his cloak, placed it in the hollow of the wall and replaced the stone before he left. The parcel contained money sent by der Flechtemann himself, to help sustain the poor of the town during the upcoming hardships.

Two soldiers walked past as he jumped back over the fence. He caught one's eye—a gaunt, sallow-eyed youth. Thinking quickly, Elias gave him a curt nod before hurriedly walking past playing children, then quickly rounding off into an alleyway. He prayed the soldier thought nothing of the incident as he hurried back to the small, closed-off miner's tunnel…his sanctuary during his stay in the city.

Elias knew he could not afford any distractions… an ambush lay afoot, and a plan was to be devised.

***

As Yakov watched the strange, black-capped man disappear into an alleyway, he knew something might be awry. He paused, wondering for a moment whether to tell Mikkel, still yammering on about a shapely girl with all the lumps and curves in the right places drawing his attention at a nearby ale house, but thought better of disturbing him. And, to that thought, he passed the cloaked man off as just another vagrant finding his way to his hole in a wall or hillside somewhere.

"…ah, but her eyes," Mikkel said with a lazy smile, before he paused to look back. "What's wrong? Did ye see somethin'?"

Yakov looked at Mikkel then, noticing his hand tighten around his spear.

"Nay, nothin'," Yakov said, unsure of why he lied.

Mikkel shot him a doubtful glance but said nothing as they continued their walk technically off-duty—only technically, though, since instructions were clear—be always on lookout.

As they made their rounds through the worn and weary streets of Schoningen, a familiar sense of unease hung in the air like a thick fog. The scars of long hunger now etched upon the faces of the people who drifted on the streets, their spirits dampened, their nails blackened. A shambling old man looked listlessly through the patrolling duo and Yakov wondered if the disheveled man saw them at all. Ever since the attempt to burn down the barracks, an ominous quiet hung in the air. Some of the men in his company, Yakov knew, overzealously usurped the urge to *correct* the dissidents. In their ire raised by the adrenalin of the moment, he witnessed one fellow soldier beating a child with the blunt end of his spear for daring to throw a pebble towards him in defense or fear; Yakov knew not which.

The narrow, winding streets were quiet and tense. Each footfall echoed like a drumbeat in Yakov's ear. Doors creaked open cautiously, revealing the barest hints of faces etched with suspicion. Turning a corner now, Yakov found himself in the market district. The once bustling marketplace now stood eerily empty, its stalls abandoned and dilapidated. The remnants of a halted economy lay scattered about as if the lifeblood of the city had simply drained away. The merchants of the city stood about in huddled groups, shooting baleful glances at Yakov and Mikkel as they passed. On the sidewalks, the gaunt and hollow-eyed poor sat begging in futile wait, knowing no one could spare even a copper token. Hunger gnawed visibly on them, and arms like kindling reached for each passerby like supplicants in a church.

Yakov knew hunger, but this was something else. His mind flashed homewards like it did so often now, carried on the tide of a dull ache throbbing in his chest. The desire to be back on the Symon landhold brought strong images of laying in tall grass under the open blue sky, in a place uncut by winding cobbles and empty lanes, untouched by spears and blood and war, unbothered by the cries of war-horns or the mutters of conspiracy. Here too much suffering to stomach eroded memories, and he wished he was anywhere, *anywhere,* but here, where even the starving looked at him with dull hate. Next to him, Mikkel did not seem so conflicted. He shot threatening glances and struck an impressive figure at each passing ruffian as though daring anyone to say anything.

"Nay o'that slouchin', Yakov," he whispered to Yakov. "Showin' frailty only invites trouble. If ye seem feeble, the toll'll be harsh. They'll probably belt a stone at your skull and leave wearing yer gambeson…yd mark my words." He paused, adding, "Stand tall and keep a hand on your pouch—nay tellin' what schemes may be afoot."

Yakov gave him an emotionless glance before complying. Increasingly, he found himself unable to understand Mikkel—the soldier standing next to him bore no resemblance to the shy young man Yakov knew only a short time ago. Mikkel now assumed the role of his own weapon of choice…his spear. He guarded Yakov fiercely, without regard for his own safety. In a way, Yakov understood…his home near Helmstedt, at least; a memory to be cherished. Mikkel knew no place as home. The faces of Anna and young Dieter were still ghostly hopes in his mind, radiant in nostalgia, but for Mikkel—well. Campfire discussions of home left Yakov to sense no visage of hope lay waiting for Mikkel.

Yakov wandered in his thoughts. *How odd, indeed. How it gnaws at the hearts of all! They suffer in misery within these city walls while I pine for the starving hardship back on the farm. Mikkel bears his own sorrow, for he hath naught to cherish in the past.* Yakov straightened his posture, chastising himself inwardly. *And here I be, mired in melancholy, for all I do is dwell on memories!*

Chapter XIV: The Ambush

"All that happens has its own reasons, whether seen they are or unseen; for the river flows unto the sea, and the rains fill the rivers. ...[So, too] is war and peace, and life and death—one occurs and causes the other, and everything has a reason. "

-Unknown Monk, circa 1382

Yakov slapped a midge-fly against the back of his neck absently, sweltering in the heat as the detachment of soldiers marched.

He and Mikkel walked with a column of men dressed for battle. His gambeson, half-hidden under a coat of suitable mail and a rather unwashed-looking tabard, only added to the misery of menacing sweat dripping down his face and neck. His unrepaired coif the result of tiredness and the constant vigilance to duty, left him opting instead for an arming-cap worn under a relatively cheap steel skullcap to prevent chaffing. A raised tuft of gambeson offered slight protection to the front of his throat from a sword-swipe—not much, but better than nothing. His legs were mostly unarmored, the rough-hide hose and dark boots offering little protection from a spear-jab or arrow. He carried his own spear, leaning at a comfortable angle against his shoulder to balance his rations, which were tied to the long haft. A cudgel and buckler, his small leather-covered wooden shield, clunked beside his thigh, creating a swinging gate most soldiers embraced as they marched.

Mikkel, slightly better equipped with his coif and a single pauldron won in a bet, was sweating even more than Yakov as they moved with the cacophony of clank and shuffle of soldiers on the move, too tired to say much else. It was an unseasonably hot day for August. Summer should have been drying out with the red trees and the aspen, but it resisted with burning glee, hateful for every soldier on march.

The company of armed men left Schoningen, what seemed to Yakov a very long week ago, on their leader's orders after a link was discovered between the dissidents within the walls and rebels outside. After a score of caravan robberies, the soldiers began a crackdown in the town and discovered a ring of rebellious spies. In the interrogations that followed, a discovery was made of two heretical spies who made good an escape from town; however, they left behind a hideout complete with a bag of stolen money, plans for further robberies, and a record of correspondence with outside agitators. Now, Niklas the Quick and Long-beard of Hesse, two of the Archbishop's most effective knights, went in pursuit with a combined host of a hundred men or so, led by a host of scouts and local trackers. They lost the runaways' trail for a while, only to pick it up again a day ago.

Rumor passed down the marching line, as rumor does, that the company of soldiers would soon be upon the enemy. Excitable gossip spread as soldiers expressed nervous, eager anticipation for bloodletting while some, as Yakov and Mikkel surmised, simply wished to get on with the task to be completed. No misconception occupied the mind of either Yakov or Mikkel of the fight to come. They were well trained to do their duty, and though very tired and weary, today would be no exception.

"How many d'ye reckon there be?" Mikkel asked, sweating.

"Can't be that many," Yakov said after a moment. "I reckon they live off the land or whatever they can shiv."

"And they certainly can't be better kitted or in better fettle'n us," Mikkel said, relaxing slightly. "We're the archbishop's holy right arm, aren't we? We sup well, train well, and are armed well. I reckon it'll just be some churls with farming gear."

Yakov gave him a look. "But you know the tales, aye? About *the man*, the one they call der Flechtemann."

Mikkel scoffed. "Old wives' tales. What, you think some arrow-carver is frolick'n about the Empire, helping the unfortunate? What, does he pick daisies for maidens too?" He chuckled.

Yakov fell silent for a moment. Another soldier in line just ahead blurted out, "Call me what y'want, but I think he's real, I do. Me brother sent word last summer…them hill bandits we used to pay tribute to…all found dead as mutton, they were. Most o' their camp nary a soul found, and the ringleaders…left to rot, with midnight arrows in their gullets." The soldier speaking paused briefly. "Musta bin tha' der Flechtemann—they say 'e ain't human, y'see."

Mikkel rolled his eyes but remained silent; Yakov, meanwhile, seemed lost in his own thoughts.

"Halt!" came word down the line as the march ground to a stop. Impatient with any delay, Longbeard, staging near the rear on horseback, now cantered past Yakov and the others on his big, shaggy draft horse, muscling the queue of soldiers aside, scowling and scolding as he worked to the front.

"Why in blazes be we halting, eh?" roared Longbeard.

A scout hurried back to meet him. "A fork in the road, sire," reported the scout upon his return, a stout local fellow with a squinted eye, his breath rasping, his voice tinged with excitement. "There be human tracks leadin' in both directions," the scout added, gesturing back the way from which he had just come. "One path wends north'ard through the woods, t'other leads east, downward to a stream, and likely beyond. Nay matter which path ye choose, caution's the word. We be on the hunt fer them rebels, aye, but word 'round these parts tells of unsavory bandits lurkin' in these woods."

Longbeard stroked his long, wavy mane, deep in thought as Niklas the Quick rode up.

"I presume you heard our conundrum," Niklas grumbled. "Should we continue up and through the woods? We may chance upon a clearing comfortable to our defense with adequate high ground to call our own."

"Or, we may prefer the replenishment for our strength by the good water of the stream?" Turning again to the scout he asked, "Tell me, man, is there a good place to camp with flat ground? A place well-defendable, where we can establish our pickets and adequately rest?"

"Oh, aye sire," the scout said, a grin on his face for being asked his opinion by a greater person than he. "There be fine, grassy ground thereat…and it be right flat, too. The stream, well, she bubbles clean and cool for a ripe distance—good, Godly water fer drinkin' and wound-cleanin'."

Niklas and Longbeard conferred. After a bit of looking up and down the path and more discussion, the two decided Niklas would go down to the stream, while Longbeard would take the other path in search of a clearing. Nodding in a final agreement, the two split their company and parted ways.

"God be praised," Mikkel panted as they trudged over a slightly downhill incline, spying the stream below. "I'd kill for a draught of good, sweet, stream-water."

"You might have to," Yakov said shortly, his knuckles white as his hand tightened on his spear. He began to feel an oppressive presence gather around the company of men—a presence he could not see, only feel. Even under the trees, the wet heat stuck clothing to their skin, making it almost unbearable to move as they marched on. Yakov, too, became suddenly aware no birds sang. The others in the column were beginning to feel this same mysteriousness also. Many shuffled their feet or stumbled while craning their necks to look nervously into the trees or the foliage of the trail around them. Shivers of unknown awareness, despite the heat, as well as uneasy murmurs ran through the line. A frustrated Niklas spurred his horse and cantered alongside them with a worried frown with Franz, his scribe, in tow, hissing at the column of men to be silent.

"Make no sound," he said in as loud a whisper as he could. "We shall take them by surprise." Whoever *they* be, he admonished himself.

"Should we nay send an envoy? Demand surrender?" Franz worried, dabbing sweat from his brow.

"In time, Franz," Niklas said in a low voice, looking about nervously before turning back to the men. Now louder as if responding to his servant in a voice of authority, assurances to his men, and more, announce to an unseen foe the intention to attack what may be nothing but shadows, he announced, "Our first attack must be swift, unseen, and brutal—only then would the threatening rabble hiding in the bushes consider surrender. Now, hold your tongues, men!"

At just that moment, there came a whooshing sound and a rustle from the nearby leaves of a bush. The gory flash of an arrow burst past Niklas' head, carving a serrated wound on his cheek in a burst of blood. He screamed, and his horse reared up, becoming difficult for him to control while acquitted with the armor and mail of his knight's badge of rank. Then, as Yakov and the others looked on in a moment of utter shock, they became aware of the arrow protruding from Franz's chest, lodging between his ribs.It was shot direct to his heart, which dropped him off his mule, dead before he hit the ground. With a cry of anguish, Niklas watched Franz's eyes cloud over.

"Ambush!" came a cry from the company line, and the men, flustered, struggled to ready their arms.

"Shield wall! Form a shield wall!" commanded the Sergeant-at-arms. In practice, the wall would be formed by the placement of shields overlapping to protect troops from the arrows of the attackers; however, the size of the soldier's buckler offered little protection in this use. As the company of soldiers tried to follow the command, in the confusion which often comes in a moment of fear where practice often flies in the face of disaster, more arrows burst through the green. Suddenly shafts sprouted from the chests of surprised soldiers, the fletching of which created an appearance of deadly flowers.

Narrowly avoiding yet another black-tufted arrow, Niklas circled to the lea side of the confusion, placing his men between him and the enemy, barking orders as tears for his fallen friend streamed down his bitter face. "Face the foe! Face the foe! Hold the line!"

A semblance of a shield wall now formed around the survivors of the attack. Yakov peered out between the small spaces left between those still able to hold their shields in the wall. Breathing hard, he took a deep breath. Action before was never like this—nothing so terrifying. Now, he felt very exposed with only his buckler for a shield. Still holding onto his spear angled forward, he struggled to remain on his feet as he stood ground in the remnants of the protective wall. His heart pounded against his ribcage, and the rhythmic thumping in his head and ears drowned out the clamor of battle. He could feel the weight of his spear in his trembling hand, its smooth wooden shaft slick with sweat. With each passing moment, the forest seemed to tighten its grip around them, its emerald canopy appeared to close in on them.

But no sooner had he and the others readied themselves facing the enemy, or so it seemed, than a fresh series of screams sounded through the forest. The guttural cry of agony pierced the air next to him. Yakov and Mikkel's eyes widened in horror, as they noticed, crumpled to the ground against Yakov's leg, a comrade, an arrow pierced through his mail, still shuddering from the impact as dark blood pooled among fallen leaves.

Recognition suddenly came to realization. "They're on both sides!" Mikkel screamed, and chaos once more broke across the line. The dense foliage seemed to taunt them, concealing their assailants, who continued to strike with deadly precision. The shield wall now in chaos, every soldier trying to find their own cover in the crossfire, Niklas the Quick, never still, galloped past his men with wild eyes, shouting commands of which no one could make any sense. Realizing he was on the verge of losing control over the entire force, Niklas roared a single command, spittle flying from his shuddering lips:

"Make for the stream!"

Though only half-heard through the screams, Niklas' words were a tenuous lifeline, a beacon of hope in the fog of battle. With a renewed purpose, the men made one final push against the torrent of panic that threatened to consume them. Now, abandoning their strained defensive line, they desperately ran down the sloping path as arrows flew past them, seeking respite in the nearby stream. Yakov's heart struggled to break free of his chest. In front of him, an arrow struck a sprinting man in the back of his calf, whereupon the man fell on his face. Barely stopping to think, Yakov jumped over him, wincing as he came down to crush the man's hand underfoot. The fallen man yelped, then screamed as he continued to be trampled in the desperate retreat.

Oh God, I'm sorry, oh God... Yakov thought as the anguish of the moment caused pain to a peer.

The stream could be seen now, bubbling ahead. The gruesome scene of battle grew utterly at odds with the serenity of the sight of the stream. Yakov, laughedmaniacally as if this relief would be his salvation by achieving a simple act. The mad laugh sprang from his lips as if simply reaching the stream would be enough to survive. The running water would somehow hold the attack of the rebels back like warlocks from children's tales. He watched as Niklas rode past Mikkel and him, ordering the remaining company to hold their ground. Beside Yakov, a wild-eyed Mikkel looked back and was nearly hit by an arrow. Glancing off his pauldron with an ugly scrape, the arrow snapped under the weight of its own impact, narrow splinters digging into his flushed neck. Mikkel cursed, tearing up, but they kept running until they reached the narrow clearing around the water source.

Now the assemblage of soldiers, their ranks less than a quarter of the beginning of the running battle, turned to face their foe, their backs to the stream. But before they could form any sort of formation whatsoever, they saw an utterly unexpected sight. A dozen bedraggled-looking horses broke through the forest, carrying on their backs hooded men carrying spears. In a single screaming charge, the small cavalry force lanced and trampled through the regiment. Spears, like venomous serpents, lanced through the air, finding their marks with ruthless precision. Blood splattered across the verdant ground and spilled into the stream, turning it crimson. Yakov and Mikkel, and those left, defended themselves as best they could using their own lances and any other weapon left to inflict as much damage as possible. Niklas the Quick attempted to rally his charges more than once before being dis-horsed by a hooded rider's lance, the lance driving into Niklas horse's chest, which reared and unceremoniously deposited Niklas on the ground.

Turning from this last vision of Niklas, who, standing in his full armor, defied the rebel horsemen, Yakov, with shaking hands, now watched as another of the horsemen bore down upon him. The rebel's faded cloak streamed behind him, a touch of blond hair visible under his hood. Gritting his teeth, Yakov howled like a feral creature before thrusting his spear at the approaching horseman—but its point missed, and the edge only cut a thin streak across the horse's muscular neck. The horse continued undeterred, whereupon the horseman's own spear slammed down against Yakov's chest where only seconds before he placed his small shield, his buckler. Yakov felt several ribs take damage through the blow to the buckler without penetrating his flesh.

In a flash of pain, Yakov found himself flying backwards, landing in the shallow stream. The shock of the cold water on his back made him choke as he grasped for breath, barely managing to roll away from the horse before it trampled him. Looking up from the crimson stream with bloodshot eyes, he saw nothing at all apart from a dim blur. All he could hear was Niklas the Quick's raspy call rising from deep within the knight's throat:

"Retreat! All retreat!"

Then everything went dark.

Chapter XV: Interrogation

"Ah, but a man holds many things even he doesn't know—and [never will], unless they are brought to the light. By the will of God, this may happen through either faith, love, or pain. If he is particularly unlucky, they'll each take a turn."

-Unknown Monk, circa 1383

The world resolved itself from the darkness like the earth being shaped at a sermon. Yakov half-watched as sensibility overcame incoherence, the heavens constructed right before his eyes, between disjointed bursts of day and night. The trees came and went. The sun rose sometimes, and as if stunned by its own heat, would disappear. Someone on the edge of conscious moments would trickle water into his mouth, only for him to be parched in the next moment.

Wakefulness drifted elusively, making consciousness wistful. Dreams came and went, and in one moment he found himself at the foot of what appeared to be a steep ravine, an impossibly long snake tied to his waist like a cord. The triangular head of the snake was reaching, always reaching, as it struggled to reach some height on the ravine walls. Over the edge of a mossy wall, Yakov could just make out a fuzzy Mikkel and Niklas looking down in concern. He opened his mouth to call to them, but with sudden pain, the snake tightened around his chest. He grimaced, aware of only passing into the stupor of the misty world between death and life, his only escape.

Fighting the pain, his head spinning, he awoke sputtering and spitting, his chest tight. The reality of the moment suddenly came rushing into the recognition of lying in the dirt, his hands tied behind him. A burning sensation rose in his chest, and wretched, kicking desperately at restraints. Just then, he felt hands behind him, pulling him roughly to his knees. His eyes burned, and he squinted at the light in front of him. Coolness and darkness to one side of him and the burning sunlight to the other brought the awareness of a cave to which his captors held him prisoner. He wobbled on his knees, cringing at his stiff neck, becoming cognizant of other men of his regiment in various states of repose or sitting against the cave wall, any wounds well-dressed and clearly tended after.

Yakov craned his neck painfully further to see the figure who held him up. Stopped in the movement to see more, another unseen hand forced him, gently but firmly, to look ahead.

"Ye daren't need look at me," came a voice behind him. "You need to look at him."

Just then, Yakov noticed another figure unnoticed before in the direction his eyes were directed. The man, partially huddled into the corner, covered in a faded, grey-green cloak, looked intently around at the captured regiment. An open hood covered most of the figure's face, hidden deep in its folds. He sat on a squat wooden chair with one leg crossed over the other. Nothing could be seen of his features with the exception that he conveyed the impression of being tall but hunched, gangly of build. The hood hid his eyes, but underneath Yakov could see hints of a rough, gaunt face through a silver-speckled, unkempt beard.

"Who…y'be?" Yakov croaked. His voice sounded foreign to his own ears.

"No one. Take him to mine lodgings," came the figure's low voice, the second instruction directed at the man behind Yakov.

"Right. Up y'go, good sir."

Yakov groaned as he was pulled to his feet, pushed along to trudge out of the cave. He blinked, half-blind in the sunlight. His eyes, still red-tinged, watered. The cave opened into a clearing in the middle of a forest, which gleamed a fresh lime-emerald in the unseasonal sun. Stern-eyed men looked at him with neutral gazes as they sat on rocks nearby sharpening their weapons or making small-talk among themselves. Not too far from the cave, Yakov could see a cheery circle of tents and a fire. Before it, he caught a glimpse of a woman who reminded him of his mother in the way she held her head and looked on into her work, stirring a pot of something. Breathing in the aroma, Yakov could almost taste what he thought might be a familiar hare-soup.

The prodding from behind did not lead to the camp, however. Removed from it, and almost immediately to the right of the cave entrance, stood a pallid grey tent, only slightly larger than others further away. A dark arrow sewn into the cloth door assumed a place with important recognition. A hand reached around Yakov and threw the cloth aside, whereupon the stern grasp of the one leading him issued him forward, compelling Yakov into the enclosed dwelling. The odor of human hygiene and old cooking created the aura of a lived-in home. Looking around the small room, he noted furs on a bed and lining the inside of the pavilion to keep in the warmth. Pushed down onto a rickety stool in the corner of the room, he continued to take in his surroundings. Near the opposite side of the room, he saw an unstrung longbow leaning against a tall, narrow-necked wicker arrow-holder. As he sought answers, the thought of escape created anxiety in his mind for both him and his captured friends.

Yakov's guard and guide now appeared in the corner of his vision, diffused by the dim sunlight entering the tent. He appeared youthful, perhaps a few years older than Yakov, with a wild shock of unruly blonde curls atop his head and a patchy, almost boyish fuzz of stubble. Despite the tension in the air, a carefree air shimmered about him as he greeted Yakov's appraising gaze with a wink.

Just as the atmosphere inside the tent was settling, the flap pushed open, and the mysterious hooded figure from earlier reentered. A glint of light from the sun off some object on the cloak of the stranger caught Yakov's eye. He noticed a brooch—it seemed to have been worked from rehammered gold, crudely made to resemble an arrow. *An arrow fer an arrow-maker,* he thought.

Memory flooded Yakov's mind, of the stories told, mostly by clergy and knights retold to men of the regiment. "Y'be der Flechtemann," Yakov said hoarsely. His mouth parched.

"Hmm. Water later, perhaps." The figure inclined his head. "Have y' now—heard of me, that is? What have ye heard?"

"That ye…" his courage grew. "Ye think y'help people. Y'think y'be a hero from the stories," Yakov blurted. He could feel a bitterness creeping into his voice, and try as he might, he could not hold back. "'Tis yer fault the townsfolk suffer. Y'give 'em hope, and they revolt against the king. Then w're sent with spears to quell the rebellion, and the home folk and their children suffer."

"And this makes *me* the origin of their suffering?" the figure asked grimly. "As ye can see, young Sieghart," acknowledging the young blond man. "It seems I be the problem all along."

The young man in the corner chuckled as der Flechtemann raised his eyes to meet Yakov's. Yakov shivered as the man's ageless green eyes seemed to pierce directly through him.

"Ye serve a monster," said the man quietly, "and I know ye know it. I hear of how he took the town—there's nothin' human in what he did."

Yakov was silent.

"But I be not here to debate with the churchman's levies," said the figure, drawing a dangerously pointed rondel dagger from his waist. He placed the point against the hollow where Yakov's neck met his collar bone. "I need information."

"W're foot-soldiers," Yakov said, looking ahead evenly. "W're told nothin. We *know* nothin."

"Nay—on the contrary, everyone knows something. Even the lowliest peasant knows that the Archbishop's a tyrant." said the man, repositioning himself to meet Yakov's stare with his unblinking gaze. "What be yer name?"

"Yakov. Yakov Symon."

A moment of silence brought about the catch of awareness in the corner of his vision. Yakov saw the blonde man look up perceptively, revealing some slight quirk of recognition. Der Flechtemann, too, watched Yakov coolly as the blonde man whispered something to him and then left the tent.

"Why did he leave?" Yakov asked, a headache beginning to build up behind his bloodshot eyes.

"Not your concern—not yet," said der Flechtemann, pulling the dagger back from Yakov's neck. "From whence d'ye hail, lad?"

"A cot to the north. Not a great way from Helmstedt." Yakov returned, still struggling to speak over a break in his voice.

The rebel leader grunted. "Volunteered fer a warband?"

"Bound by contract t'service." Yakov said, suspiciously eyeing his captor.

Der Flechtemann was quiet for a moment, then said, "Speak…tell me of the leader of thine troop. Few have felt my arrows and lived to tell the tale."

"Niklas…Niklas the Quick, our knight's name, it be. He…he be not a bad man. A good leader…and we followed," Yakov stammered, remembering him circling wildly in the forest, rallying the regiment to stand strong. "Our knight tried to stay the hand of the Abbot, but it availed him naught." Yakov stared into some parcel of space beyond der Flechtemann, sighed, and then focused on the rebel leader's eyes. "Much blood colored the field as a result, but the stain remains with Niklas the Quick." He recounted with nauseating distaste for the archbishop.

Der Flechtemann looked at him without response, and Yakov found it difficult to tell what thoughts lay behind the piercing eyes.

"So, Niklas survived?" Yakov asked suddenly.

"Aye, he did. A goodly number of thy men were able to flee the field because of him. He be one of the better leaders I have seen in a noble's army." der Flechtemann said grudgingly. "Half of them become petty lordlings who care nay if their men live or die, so long as they can slink away. The other half," he curled his lip, "are jackals fer hire—mercenaries. Unprincipled lackeys who serve only their own interests, without even the semblance of loyalty or honor. Naught any good can be expected from such scavengers."

Yakov's mind flashed to a past remembrance of the Chain's grinning face, and he found himself agreeing internally with the rebel. *Niklas might be one of the men who served the Abbot, but that be nay positive reflection of the Abbot himself, a man who regularly employed knights to do his bidding, monsters like Petres.* He thought.

The mesmerizing countenance of der Flechtemann caught Yakov off guard. "The Abbot," Yakov heard himself quietly saying, "he has mercenaries on his payroll. One of them—one of them is bad. The most terrible man I've known. They call him the Chain. Petres the Chain." His feelings of the past few years came tumbling out, released in torrent of thoughts and visions of the insanity he kept hidden in his mind's eye.

Der Flechtemann leaned forward suddenly, his eyes keenly alive. "Petres the Chain—the mercenary bandit knight? That butcher? Aye, I know him. He been waylayin' merchant trains, settin' fire to fields, and leavin' a path of carnage 'cross Duke Magnus's land." Der Flechtemann paused in thought, stood, and turning back to Yakov, asked, "Ye say he be in the Abbot's employ?"

"Aye, he is."

"And ye be certain, lad?"

"With certainty, aye,;he be the one who brought me to the Abbot and sold me into servitude." Yakov said, relieved.

Der Flechtemann leaned back, his long fingers twisting the curls and snarls of his unkempt beard. His eyes seemed far away. "This be ill news. By repute, the man serves as a creature of the abyss—a creature born of night and malice." The rebel leader said in disgust. His angst suddenly turning to urgency, "Once word of our raid reaches the Abbot, he will unleash his hound of hell upon us without a moment's hesitation."

He was right, and Yakov knew it. The Chain would jump at this chance to quash these rebels. Money a non-necessity, the sport of the chase and the kill created an addictive attraction for the Chain. The rebels would provide him with plenty of that, and so Petres would drop anything to come here if the Abbot were to ask. As Yakov observed the rebel leader's countenance quietly, a strange sense of familiarity ate at him as the man sat hunched in thought.

Without warning, the tent door flew open, and in stepped the blond rebel who left earlier. The abrupt appearance of the man startled Yakov.

"Sieghart?"

"If ye be done with him," the young man said, "she wants to see him right away."

"Ah. Would she bide her time if I said nay?"

"Forgive me, sire, but I fear she would simply burst in." Der Flechtemann sighed again, before looking at Yakov.

"Go on, then. Get out." The rebel leader waved Yakov out with his hand.

"Who calls for me?" Yakov asked, suddenly guarded.

"Out," repeated der Flechtemann. "I need to mull this over…but we'll talk again, lad. Y'd better try to think of anything else ye might know."

Nodding hesitantly, Yakov rose on unsteady feet, stumbling past the seated rebel leader as he made to exit the tent. The young man—Sieghart—held the flap open as Yakov existed, blinking in the bright sun. His eyes watered, and he wiped a forearm against them.

***

When he blinked his eyes back open, he saw the woman seen earlier—the one who reminded him so oddly of his mother, standing nearby under a tree, hands clasped before her. She wore a humble dress and a green cloth shawl that covered her hair entirely but for two long, flaxen braids that fell to either side of her chest. Bright eyes looked at him, as he reddened behind his own uncontained tears.

"*Anna?* Be it ye?" Yakov said, dumbfounded.

She broke into sobs and rushed at him. Stunned, he could only stand with arms held stiffly outstretched as she hugged him tight, her sobbing face buried in his chest. Dumbly, all he could think of was how short she seemed now. "Who cut your feet from under ye? Y'er so small," he remarked.

"My Yakov," she said, stepping back to hold his face in her work-roughened hands. Her wet eyes overflowed. "My little Yakov. I thought…I thought I'd never—"

"What be goin' on?"

Yakov looked in the direction of the voice, nearly doing a double take. He felt like he was looking at himself as a boy, though this youth wider now in the shoulders, with his hair sullenly middle-parted. The youth stood like a

197

startled deer, glancing from one face to the next in confused panic.

"Dieter?" Yakov asked, still in a strange, far-away voice. "Be that ye, tiny Dieter?"

The boy squinted, and then his eyes widened. *"Brother?"*

"Aye Dieter," Anna managed, still crying. "Tis yer brother."

Turning back to Yakov she continued, "When they told me ye'd been taken from Helmstedt, I be…I didn't know what to…"

"I don't understand," Yakov said faintly. "Why aren't ye at the farm? What happened? Why…?"

"He doesn't seem well," Sieghart observed, throwing an arm around Yakov's shoulders as his vision swayed. "Here, put yer weight on me shoulder." He said stepping between Yakov and Anna. "Give him some space to breathe, Anna, love."

The display of affection between the two barely registered with Yakov. He felt strangely feverish, and putting his weight on the helpful rebel, tried to limp towards the campfire with his siblings in tow.

Reality slipped in and out of his tired mind. In the delirium between rest and confusion he could remember the promise he had made to return home, but this was not home… or was it?

Chapter XVI: The Choice

"The Seeker Seeks for he hopes to find. But some men may find what they'd never thought to seek. They then may accept or reject revelation— but a point about revelation. It is never ignored."

-Unknown Monk, circa 1384

Yakov sat, his back to a tree, looking unseeing into the distance where, past the swaying trees, the mountains were half-visible. Their steep sides rose from the dull morning fog like giants now awakening, ignited on one side by the scintillant golden sun.

"So, mum's passed then?" he asked finally.

In front of him, on the grass, Anna and Dieter sat. Out of earshot—but not too far away—Sieghart stood with arms crossed ostensibly to keep an eye on Yakov and ensure he not create a commotion or attempt an escape.

But then, he surmised Yakov showed no intention to attempt anything so idiotic in this surrounding. Sitting against a tree with his gangly legs stretched out, restricting leather armor long since peeled away from his tunic, and hose, Yakov now presented a picture of vulnerability. His eyes, still bloodshot, were glassy, and his sweat-slick hair stuck to his forehead from bodily exertion and the beating heat.

"She…there were no pains," Anna said, not knowing what else to say. She knew Yakov to be the closest of the children to their mother. Anna felt no explanation could contribute meaningfully in telling him his mother died soon after he left, partially in grief of his parting, and partially in the sickness racking her body. Sick as their mother was, no staying behind would have bolstered the situation at the farmstead. Bills needed to be paid, and Yakov set out to do just that. The drunkenness of Uncle Karl and his pension to gamble caused the farm to fall in arrears. No fault could be set on Yakov, but he took the step as the eldest male determined to bring rest to the problem.

Dieter, absently twisting a blade of grass around his finger, suddenly spoke up. "I don't remember her."

Yakov looked at him for a moment, reminded of Mikkel. With sad eyes, he told Dieter, "She loved thee, lad. Y' were always afraid of being in the room. Y'often hid behind Anna while mum's sickness showed terrible, but she loved ye."

Dieter didn't reply, and they were quiet for a moment.

Yakov's eyes now focused back to Anna. "So, y' left Karl the farm?" Yakov said, blinking his eyes as if to clear his vision.

"Aye, our uncle got only worse after ye left." Anna said quietly. "I became afraid he'd hurt Dieter. Then, when Sieg and his folk showed up—"

"Y' mean the rebels," Yakov said, anger in his voice, showing contempt from having been taken prisoner.

Anna frowned in her own stubbornness toward Yakov. "Rebels or no, they're the reason we be safe today."

"Safe?" Yakov laughed bitterly. "Ye be a member of a group rebellin' against the Reichskrone. One day or the next, thee'll all be rounded up, strung up by thy necks and left to hang and rot. Y'think this be *safe?*" he finished with a loud retort, staring now at his sister.

"Well, they've survived this far," Anna snapped with equal compulsion, "an' they made short work of the army that held ye captive."

As Yakov's hollow gaze settled on her, Anna immediately regretted her words. The weight of whatever terror lay in his past now tainted her understanding of him. The last few years lay heavy on his eyes, and her heart broke to remember the carefree youth who agreed to go to Helmstedt for all their sakes. No boyish joy showed in his eyes now. These were the eyes of a man living in the pain of hideous remembrances of sights he could not set aside. She could see the duties he performed in the Abbot's name polluted the ambitions set out so nobly in his youth. Yakov was back, true, but not the Yakov she and Dieter knew as younger siblings.

"It be not only about the holy church and the Diet, 'twas it? The Archbishop and the indulgences collected by the clergy affect all." Yakov said softly. "Ye really believe in the cause of these people…these rebels…in their der Flechtemann."

Anna shifted awkwardly. "Aye, I do. 'Tis hard to believe. But 'tis true." She gently moved towards Yakov and took his hands in hers. "They've welcomed us open-armed and treated us like we be one of their own." Anna continued, trying to reason with him. "These people *understand* us, more than any nobleman or taxman or census-officer. They know what it be like to work the land, to sweat in the sun, and to worry about our families. Most come from the same station of birth as we, an' they fight for what they believe." She dropped his hands and turned away in exasperation at his stare. She was not sure if she was connecting with him. Turning back, she said, "They care, Yakov. They truly care."

"And y'care for them, too," Yakov said, looking at Sieghart in the distance, his temper beginning to relax. The man gave him a short wave and a smile. Looking back at Anna, he acknowledged the smile she tried to hide. "Y' love that one, don't ye?"

Anna blushed, and Dieter laughed. He whispered to her with the old needling smile, "It's obvious."

Anna mumbled something, and Yakov managed a quick, quiet comment expressing something close to a smile. He turned away, privately troubled; the fact his sister's love for this rebel hardly boded well. But the truth in what she said began to seep into his awareness. *I've known it, aye,* he thought. *The greed of merchants, the monstrous capacity of Papal representatives, the brutality of mercenaries, and the coldness of them nobles.* All of them had brought about ugly memories of the last few years he now kept in his heart.

Being used as an instrument of a status quo which he had found not to his liking, brought up anger and, at the same time, a terrible sadness. Sadness in the fact he found himself in this place instead of on the homestead accomplishing his intention. Anger at his drunk uncle Karl, corrupt tax collectors, Jon and Ingemar, the conniving merchant Adelman, the rogue knight Petres the Chain, and finally, Longbeard of Hesse and Niklas the Quick all lent their part in his unfocused run to the present, straying farther and farther away from the original promise to return. *How long ago did I make the decision to help the farm and family…six years? Seven years?* He rethought the mix of emotions of his present captivity. *It be a terrible thing for one to be the sword of the oppressor, to be the boot designed to stamp on the common man.*

Leaning his head back against the tree, Yakov suddenly remembered an image from the slaughter at Schoningen, an image his mind almost succeeded in forgetting: a youth with bedraggled hair, scarcely more than fourteen summers, standing with wide eyes, holding his own guts. In his hands, Yakov's spear was stained red, its tip shaking as the youth fell sideways, glistening bloody knots spilling onto the cobbles. Yakov shut his eyes as tight as he could, his breathing hard, gorge rising in his throat and he placed the image in the farthest part of his mind. He coughed and spit bile on the ground at his feet.

Dimly, he could hear Anna's worried voice: "Yakov? Yakov, are ye well? Dieter, call—no, go fetch Werner! Sieg! Help me with Yakov!"

Yakov coughed, holding up a hand. "Nay! Just water, please… I'm well, I just—"

But his protests were useless. As he tried to resist the effort, his sister and the rebel Sieghart were insistent on finding him comfort. Soon, Dieter returned with a balding old man who leaned over Yakov, prodding at his throat and sides with bony hands. The man, a grizzled old herbalist named Werner, knew well the signs of a troubled heart and mind, and the unseen wounds that lingered long after the blood and sweat dried. A furrowed brow accompanied his examination, and Yakov wondered if the man had children. He looked every bit like the disapproving father.

"Well," Werner began, his voice hoarse. "There's neither illness of humors, nor the bite of an ill insect which torments this 'un. Whatever be within thee, boy, 'tis nay a flesh wound." Peering at Yakov, he continued. "This be a malady o' the soul."

"What are ye, a priest now?" Sieghart frowned, leaning to look at Yakov. "What do y' mean 'o' the soul'?"

Yakov's gaze shifted slightly between Werner and Sieghart. "I'm good," he said. "I'm well now—I can move."

"I don't doubt it," old Werner said grimly, and without another word began to walk away. As Anna and Dieter hovered over Yakov, Sieghart caught up to the old herbalist.

"What was that?" Sieg asked, exasperated. "Speak plainly, old man. What troubles him?"

The old man, peering up at Sieghart, sighed and commented, tilting his head to one side in diagnosis. "His wounds be healing well, lungs be unbruised, humors seem balanced. Neither jaundice in his cheek, nor slackness in the jaw causes any concern t'me. No malady in 'is blood either, but the illness, I recollect, comes from his soul…it may never go. 'Tis war weariness which comes, and I seen a young 'un come back from the wars with it in 'is heart, and 'e carried it till 'is dying day."

Sieghart looked back at the gangly figure stretched out on the grass trying to sit up, and chuckled. Anna, her hair hanging over her face, tried to keep Yakov lying down. Entertained, he turned back to the old herbalist.

"Would 'e die of it?" Sieg asked carefully.

"Oh, nay," the old man shrugged. "Not likely, such things be in the domain of the Lord above. But I'll wager a farthing he be a man haunted for sure. A conjuror or a priest's prayer may bring remedies for wounds unseen, I've heard tell, but neither balm nor splint can be of much use for such illness as this. All a man like he can do is laugh occasionally and forget what he can."

Sieg sat on his haunches, feet flat to the ground and considered for a moment a response. To Warner he simply said, "Well, we need 'im in good health."

The old man nodded without a word and left, leaving Sieg looking at the siblings again from a distance.

***

The next day, and Yakov's condition was improving. He sat in the periphery of the camp with Dieter, and the brothers accompanied eachother in comfortable silence, watching others around the camp joke amongst each other.

At the fire, Anna was busy throwing chopped wild onions into her stew. Other open fires were scenes of similar activity where women busied themselves in the cooking of the meal. A few children played close by. Soon the sweetness of the onion added to the fragrance of the broth Anna boiled.

"Never thought I'd see our Anna fitting in with rebels," Yakov said, then chuckled, remembering life together as siblings. "But then again, she always been rightly feisty." After all, Anna had taken responsibility for the boys when their father left. Yakov continued. "If they put a sword in her hands, the Abbot would have his hands full." The two brothers laughed.

Dieter conveyed a simple smile, though it wore off. "She tried, at one point…t'persuade them. To let her fight with them, that is."

"And?" Yakov asked, a knot in his throat. Jokes aside, no risk could assuage a desire for his sister to never know war.

"Sieg wouldn't allow it," Dieter said, giving him a sidelong glance. "Lets her hunt for game a-times, but he's never let her come on a raid. He…well, y've seen how he looks at her. He worries for her, which be fine by me."

"And with me," Yakov sighed. "What of ye? Have they asked ye to…?"

"Nay," Dieter said. "I'd say Anna asked them not to let me fight."

"I'd have done the same," Yakov said, then paused at the peeved look by Dieter. "What? Ye want to fight?"

"I'd like the choice at least," Dieter said hotly, then looked away. "Everyone deserves to choose, at least."

"Aye, but few get to choose. And either way, y'd hardly be free in battle," Yakov said with a grim smile. "A soldier is a slave, just by another name. The fruit of battle is blood, and blood's finest within a man's livin' veins, not won and spilt on grass."

Dieter gave him a doubtful look, but before he could say anything, there was a cough behind them. They turned to see Sieghart standing there apologetically. He nodded to Yakov, then shot a look over at der Flechtemann's tent.

"He's been asking for ye," Sieg said, offering Yakov his hand.

Yakov took it, and the rebel pulled him up. Yakov begrudgingly allowed himself a moment of appreciation for the man. He seemed like the good sort—at least, more easily readable than his commander, the enigmatic figure heralded by an arrow. Clapping Dieter on the back, Yakov gingerly followed Sieghart through the tall grass, one hand absent-mindedly brushing past the tree-trunks, like he used to as a child. Looking at the trees around him, he felt a twinge of sadness for those wonderful days spent by himself in the countryside, when he would run off the farm in the morning and return late to a scolding by Anna or a beating from Karl. Of course, he would do it all over again—those moments of peace meant everything to him.

"You feelin' well, friend?" Sieg asked, his stance prepared, as though to catch Yakov if he fell.

"I'm well," Yakov replied as der Flechtemann's tent drew nearer. "At some point, we'll talk about you and my sister."

"Ah," Sieg said, pausing awkwardly. "Look, Yakov, there be nothing…"

"Peace, friend," Yakov said with a smile. "Dieter told all, and I believe ye be a good man—but a brother worries. Ye understand."

Sieghart nodded; as always, the subject of Anna tended to reduce the usually eloquent rebel to a lovestruck boy. As they neared the tent, Sieg noticed the smile fall from Yakov's face, a look of worry replacing it.

"Worry not," Sieghart whispered with a reassuring smile. "He seems more terrifyin' than he be."

Yakov gave him a slight nod and made to enter—but then a voice called from their right, "Here, Sieg. Bring him here."

They followed the voice to find der Flechtemann sitting some way behind the pavilion on a naturally raised platform of stone, half covered in tufted threads of long grass and a coat of rich moss. Atop it, sat der Flechtemann, stringing his longbow without expression, his hood pulled back, and his gray hair roughly shorn short, as though with a dull knife. His face, rugged and rough, betrayed no trace of emotion or strain as he bent the firm longbow into shape with tough, sinewy arms. He nodded to Yakov and gestured at Sieghart to leave. With a reassuring nod, the young rebel left.

"He be a good boy," der Flechtemann said in an even voice. "But soft, in some ways. He doesna' understand war, not really. He knows enough to fight, aye, but he be comforted by our cause. He be comforted acuz he hath choice—he choose to fight, and so he be content in battle. *Ye didna' have a choice—and so ye know war.*"

Yakov leaned against a nearby tree, looking at the rebel leader curiously. "Y'speak like a man with no choice."

"I don't," der Flechtemann said simply. "I have nay choice. I chose once, aye—but now, no choice remains. I belong to the cause, and it runs through me. It guides me arm. It guides me arrows."

"Then, who guides the cause?" Yakov asked.

"A good question. The people, ideally," der Flechtemann replied, a hint of irony in his voice. "But then, a-times, the people must be guided to recognize their chains. The chains run deep, y'see—the people do not often see'm, unless in times of poverty, sickness, or war."

"Luckily for you, sir," Yakov said sardonically, "This be the age of all three. The crops die and stomachs starve while men like me march in the name of noble blood. And here ye are, with yer arrows and promises—could ye truly promise to win against the crown?"

"I promise nothing," der Flechtemann said. "For I have nothing to promise. I be a man like ye, a man like them," he nodded towards the camp, "And a man like every other farmer, yeoman, and commoner. All I offer be a cause, a chance, and the same choice I once made."

"And what choice be that?"

"The choice to act or the choice to ignore," the rebel leader said, as though it were the most natural choice in the world. "Most do not know there be another path—my duty be to show them the fork in the road. Continue along the straight path or take the path less travelled. In the end, ye'll be defined by the path, but ye may still choose the path to be enslaved by."

"A slave to other men, or a slave to a cause," laughed Yakov. "That be yer choice?"

Der Flechtemann raised an eyebrow. "Correct."

Yakov was silent. No argument or defense came from the rebel. No grand speeches of noble causes, or cruelties like the mercenaries imposed with hot irons or arrows shot into flesh. No self-righteous piety like the clergy came in the discussions between Yakov and the leader of this cause. Yakov found himself perplexed, yet warming to an understanding of this man, der Flechtemann, this strong leader. At every turn, this man confounded Yakov's expectations…in some ways, Yakov found himself thinking, der Flechtemann was more a monk than the actual monks met by himself in his work for the knights of the Abbot. Der Flechtemann was a man dedicated to something greater, a man who seemed genuinely selfless, to the point where it was impossible for Yakov to see him as anything but his cause.

"My sister believes in ye," Yakov said after a pause. "As does young Dieter. So, what be your game here? Be ye offerin' me thy beloved choice as well?"

"I have no *game,* only requirements. All I need from ye, lad," der Flechtemann said, "Be information."

"I told you I know nothing of their plans."

"But y'*do* know of the local supply routes," der Flechtemann said. "Ye must," the leader grilled. "I be told the garrison often sent out sorties to escort caravans along the routes. Truth?"

It was true. Yakov did not bother to ask the rebel how he knew so much—clearly, the town's dissident elements were well in touch with the rebels, and in far greater numbers than the Abbot assumed.

"I know the routes," Yakov said, "but what do ye intend to do with them? I told ye, the Abbot will likely summon his dog back from his bloodletting. Petres the Chain *will* come here, and he *will* hunt ye down for both coin and blood."

"Ye leave the strategy to me, lad," came the calm reply. "Give me what I ask fer."

"Fine," Yakov said. "I'll tell ye."

"A good choice," der Flechtemann said, inclining his head. "See my scouts before sundown; explain the routes to them. They're more familiar with this region than I."

Yakov nodded and made to leave. But then he paused, and looked back at the leader of the rebels, who was testing the draw of the longbow he had just strung.

"I see why ye didn't offer me a choice," Yakov said wryly. "There be no choice for me, be there? My sister wants to be with your man Sieghart. My uncle probably sold our farm now that nought one be working at it. We don't have anywhere else to go. I could go back to the Abbot's forces, but the wages the Chain got for us be far less than volunteers; I couldn't keep Anna and Dieter fed on them. I know nay craft, either. I have nay choice but t'be your man."

"As ye said," der Flechtemann said quietly. "All we can choose be a cause to be enslaved by. Y've simply had slightly less choice than most."

Yakov laughed grimly and left.

Chapter XVII: The Hunt

"God preserve the helpless beast. The elk, [red]eyed, flees the hunter; it is the beloved of God, fleeing his Man on Earth; it is the voice of the helpless...torn down by the whims of the two-legged and unwise."

-Unknown Monk, circa 1382

Yakov mindlessly picked a filament of gristle from his teeth as he looked listlessly into the dark, snowy trees. Dieter and Anna sat on either side of him, and all three were dressed for travel. Yakov's cloak, and warm clothes had been returned by Anna, but it did not make the winter any less brutal. It struck with cruel intensity. As they huddled together for shared warmth, they watched shadows in the ebony black before them, their breath fogging through parted, shivering lips.

The trio wished for the warmth of a fire, but watchful standby afforded them invisibility and the cunning to move quickly. Sieghart stood a short distance away, waiting for one of their scouts, a day late, to return. Der Flechtemann, worried, sent two pickets to look for their advanced spotter when apprehension of discovery by an enemy reared its ugly head. Now the company of resistance fighters sat quietly in the cold darkness anticipating the next move.

The protected supply route movement given up to the rebels a long four months ago by Yakov brought der Flechtemann's prediction true. Petres the Chain, called back from his post as countryside bandit knight, set out to hunt the rebels like a hungry dog. Cruelty to the local villagers became the norm as this vicious knight forced testimony though corruption of the common good and maligning public officials to give up the names of conspirators.

Creating diversion and change in tactics, the rebels evaded the knight and his mercenaries with cunning and illusion, hitting various supply lines randomly with quick raids from hiding and then disappearing as if never there aided the evasion. Captured goods and treasures from raids trickled in and out of camp, and Yakov, to his surprise, learned much of the wealth was consigned and transported back to Schoningen; however, the delivery point now painted the picture of a most unusual receptor. Funds and merchandise taken in raids from the Abbot and his cronies found their way to the same location taken as taxes and there to be dispersed. Yakov knew well the portion to anyone would mean only a paltry sum once divided amongst the people. Der Flechtemann's advance man in the town, a scout named Elias, ensured the distribution was carried out fairly.

Now, as they shivered, Sieghart paced to and fro, shooting nervous glances toward der Flechtemann's hooded figure. The personage stood some distance away with his gray bay, accompanied by two more archers dressed almost exactly like him. As Anna stifled a yawn and Yakov continued to look around camp, Dieter stood up and checked the reins on the horses for the fifth time. Yakov looked at his brother closely. Unlike Yakov at that age, Dieter was uncommonly quiet, given to a silent anxiety that was never worded, but was always visible. A worrier by nature, Yakov knew; the boy sometimes reminded him of an old man.

The silence was suddenly broken by a rustle in the bushes. Immediately, the rebels tensed. Hands wandered close to quivers, while bows were lifted. Breaking through the shrubbery, lit by the dull, diffused chilling moonlight, the two pickets emerged, pale and winded. Sieg immediately sprang into action, going to confer with them.

"Well?" he asked, looking at each in turn. "Where be Eugen?"

"We found 'im," said one man, ghostly pale and sweating. "Or most of 'im. They quartered 'im, Sieg.

"Aye, drawn an' quartered, 'e was." said the other man, his jaw clenched. "Yonder be three quarters hangin' from the trees, used fer target practice." He said, waving his hand above his head, "the fourth one, well... we reckon it musta fell down, and some wolf or other dragged it off."

"S'blood," Sieghart muttered. "How far?"

"Twas five hours a-travelling we did, but they be likelier further afield, so twill take them longer. Most of 'em ain't got no horses, so they'll be walking for a day at least."

"Pox," Sieg cursed, his voice filled with frustration and grief.

"What is it?" asked der Flechtemann in a low voice as he strode over.

"Eugen's dead," Sieg repeated with vitriolic disgust. "The Chain's done him in, quartered him like a beast. Though his message be clear, that bloody Petres will pay the price."

The message, Yakov knew, was *ye'll be next.*

The weight of their comrade's fate settled heavily upon the rebels. Well liked around the camp, Eugen had carried a cheerful demeanor about him. His bowl of auburn hair and unruly beard set him apart, and Yakov knew a man like this could carry the humor of the company a long way towards good morale. Meeting such a violent end seemed out of place for Eugen. The Chain's mercenaries hounding the partisan group knew no bounds, and the Abbot's desire to crush the rebels by freeing his dog, Petres the Chain, to whatever means necessary, only emboldened his followers.

Sieg's mind raced with thoughts of revenge. A long hatred for the methods of the church now burned even brighter within him, enshrined in the fire of defiance. No capitulation of any revenge would suffice—yet he knew rushing into action without a plan would only lead to more lives lost.

"I be weary unto death," der Flechtemann said loudly, looking around at the assembled rebels, "But we must be quick about it. We shall make a strike to the north, to the supply route that enters the town from the north. Mourning for our fallen brother must wait. Prepare what ye need, for we leave soon. Eugen's sacrifice shall not be in vain."

The rebels dispersed, making their final adjustments to saddles and supplies in the shadows, their worried faces lost in the darkness of the night. Without another word, der Flechtemann began to walk back to his horse, shadowed by a worried looking Sieg. As they passed the siblings, der Flechtemann gestured to Yakov.

"With me, boy," he said, and Yakov agreed with a nod.

As they walked to the secluded bay, der Flechtemann turned to look at Yakov. "Ye want to say something."

"'Tis a trap," Yakov said flatly. "Ye think the chain be some simpleton? Nay, he's no fool, that one. Cunning as a wily wolf he be, and thrice as wretched. Every damn instance he's caught ye, thou managed to slip from his grip, hittin' our stockpiles where it hurts instead. Petres, he knows right well the blasted northen route's the only path untouched by yer strikes." Pausing briefly, he continued with a side glance to der Flechtemann. "And ain't it a peculiar twist we've been marchin' north these past five sunrises?"

"Aye," der Flechtemann said, stroking his beard with one hand, contemplating a response. "Mark my words, he'll be anticipatin' our move onto the northen pat. I wager he'll be plottin' an ambush, snug-like, close to yonder thicket. It's prime ground to ensnare any supply-laden wagons makin' their way townward," he spoke with a resolute air. "Me own roots lie in the north, and back when our fellowship was just takin' form, we spent a fair stretch in them parts. It stands to reason, he'd position his lot uphill from us, waitin' until he's rightly certain we've ventured deep into the woods. Then, come nightfall—"

"He'd slit our throats while we slumber." said Sieghart somberly.

"He's like to come a-chargin' straight inta our camp." Yakov spat with a touch of resentment. "'Tis his favored gambit for layin' traps. Come sundown, they'll take the path till the shroud of night, then come thunderin' through the foe's own camp, ridin' tall on their steeds, trampin' good men and all beneath them hooves of theirs. Those as didn't meet their end by the blade'd be skewered or bludgeoned, mark me words."

Sieg shuddered. "Beast! What shall we do now? We cannot continue northward."

"North is exactly where we go," said der Flechtemann, mounting his horse. "And we'll ambush his ambush."

"Wha'?" Yakov asked, his eyes wide.

"We curve around the hills," said their leader, looking down at Yakov with his typically deadpan face. "Scale the far side and rain down upon them like the wrath of God!"

"I grasp thine intent," Sieghart spoke cautiously, "but truth be told, we ain't certain if they'll be makin' camp amidst yonder hills. We might find ourselves assailin' naught but trees."

"We'll need to scout, aye," said der Flechtemann, "This be an opportunity, for they think to have us trapped in their cunning snare, but they know not we be foxes, not sheep," he remarked quietly, placing a mind's-eye finger alongside his nose. "We shall slip through their grasp and leave them scratching their heads. We play fox to outwit that unhallowed miscreant."

"Aye. And I daresay that winding about the hills shal take us out of Petres" sight," Sieghart mused, nodding with understanding. "We must needs move with speed and stealth. Any scouts we send forth to espy the foe's movements must be our finest."

"'Tis madness," said Yakov, looking from der Flechtemann to Sieg. "Ye ain't laid eyes on how the Chain unleashes his brutal tricks in battle. He be a beastly terror even to a greenhorn, let alone to one schooled in the ways. He be mastered his art, mind ye—reckon a simple soul could lead his lot to march with such haste as to confound ye in chase and lay down a devilish trap to snare ye unawares?" Yakov reasoned. "D'ye reckon this savage would've shied from confrontin' the disciplined troops of the Duke all these days?"

"I trust he be cunning," der Flechtemann said calmly. "I count upon-it; and as fer having seen the Chain's warband at their craft—ye've seen my men focused in action." The leader continued, "Say then, wilt thou not say our arrows would pierce the merciless hearts of the Chain's lot?"

Yakov, quiet for a moment, questioned, "What of Anna and Dieter? What of the old, and the commoners among us?"

"Aye, camp followers and the like shall not ambush anyone," Sieg said quickly, before looking at der Flechtemann for affirmation. The man nodded wryly.

"Don't worry, lad," der Flechtemann said. "Thy brother and sister shall be safe—and many like them shall be safer still once this cur is put to the sword."

Despite himself, Yakov felt a spark of hope in the gloom. Remembrances of the Chain's brutality, recalling firsthand, brought gorge to his throat. The thought of turning the tables on this corrupt knight and his horde was a beacon of hope here in a pit-filled darkness.

"A whit of me be fain," Sieg said with a sigh, echoing Yakov's worrisome feelings. "I liked Eugen well. His good humor will be sorely missed around camp." With a more argent expression to his response, he continued." An if e'er I get a chance, I'll flay that bastard Petres meself. That'll be justice done."

Der Flechtemann nodded wryly in agreement. "Aye, justice it shall be," he said, "Let the Chain and his curs suffer of their own game! I doubt they'll find our arrowheads to their liking."

Yakov nodded hesitantly, and the impromptu council broke apart. Returning to his siblings, he told them to mount.

"We know to where they head," Sieg announced to the rest of the camp, relaying der Flechtemann's orders, his voice carrying the weight of leadership. "We be off now. The plan be to waylay not another caravan, but Petres the Chain himself." Surprise murmured across the rebels, and der Flechtemann stepped up himself, still atop his horse. A hesitant quiet now quelled the mumble of his company of patriots.

"Eugen's memory will guide us," he said in the hushed silence afforded him. "Nay be these misbegotten churls and nobles and prelates unlike us, we remember our own. We shall ne'er forget their sacrifice, the blood they shed for the love of freedom. Every comrade lost in this struggle be a part of the cause they died for. In each shaft we loose, we send forth the courage and dreams of our kin."

The night air hung heavy with the collective sorrow and determination of the rebels. Yakov looked around him and saw a camaraderie he never saw in neither the Chain's warband nor the Abbot's army. Among the rebels the fallen lived on through the memories of their brethren. The thought of avenging the deaths of their comrades seemed to add fuel to the fire burning within each partisan's soul.

"Assembled, ye've witnessed grievous loss. Ye've felt depths of pain beyond reckonin'," der Flechtemann's voice carried, his gaze searching the unwavering images of his men. "Nay, ye've also tasted boundless unity. Brotherhood. A tie of kin that be stronger than the Rhine's current. Yon scoundrel Petres thinks his blade shall shatter us, break them ties, and scatter us like dust in the gale. But that shall not come to pass. Fer every soul felled by death, we bear his vision onward, still."

Sieghart nodded, his heart swelling with emanate resolve. Many around him stirred, raising their heads with rancor. Yakov understood their thoughts. The partisans believed they were not mere pawns in a power struggle, they were warriors with a divine purpose. Their cause was just, this they assured themselves. They rallied around der Flechtemann not only to fight for themselves and the anguish each felt, but for all those who suffered under the iron grip of the Reichskrone.

Yet we hath nary a choice but to place our faith here, Yakov thought, and he knew der Flechtemann knew it. *Having come thus far,* he reflected, *the purpose must stand foremost in our thinking.*

"So, as we march, we seek not only vengeance's pursuit—but justice's verdict." der Flechtemann said, his jaw clenched. "May Petres render the toll for his blood-shedding. May the Chain be rent asunder."

The night air seemed to crackle, and as they cheered and nodded, the rebels suddenly seemed to stand tall, ready to face the trial that lay ahead. In the face of daunting odds, Yakov wondered at der Flechtemann's ability to rouse his men. It seemed strange to him a man should believe in a cause so strongly he would willingly walk into the mouth of the lion out of sheer trust.

Under the cover of the moon, they began their silent ascent, climbing the opposite side of the hills, shrouded in the darkness that favored their purpose. Several wagons and the noncombatants were left at the foot of the hills with a taciturn rebel named Ludomir to guard them.

As they made to part, Yakov hugged Anna and ruffled Dieter's hair.

"Why do y'have to go?" Anna said bitterly. "Y'won't even be fightin'."

"He ain't voiced it," Yakov let out a breath, "but I reckon they still ponder if I be takin' 'em into a trap. He be a wary one, this der Flechtemann. There be always a safety net in his schemes, I'd wager."

Anna looked away unhappy, while Yakov joined the rebels as they began their ascent. A solemn air pervaded among the rebels as the cold night bit into their bones. Yet despite the painful cold, the fate of their beliefs, the memory of Eugen, and the hope for a better future pushed the partisan band forward. They moved like whispers in the wind on this moon-filed night, an unseen fury, poised to strike like the vengeance of God upon those who dared to oppress them.

***

As dawn broke, Sieg gathered the rebels together, their faces somber, blowing warmth into cold hands, some warming their hands in their armpits. Eugen's memory and the method of his execution still weighed heavily on their minds. Determined to bring down the Reichskrone tyranny, their hearts united in the shared purpose. The time came now and would soon come to pass to strike with vengeance… to strike hard.

Der Flechtemann sat at the head of their camp, his hood thrown up while resting, standing in the back of a wagon. He looked across the expectant faces of his men and nodded.

"We be set to strike 'em where we can drive a wedge'" spoke the commander in a hushed tone. "To lure 'em into aidin' our scheme to cut at the heart of their maraudin' champion, the Chain. We be in want of a commotion to draw their eyes away."

Sieg frowned. "What sort of commotion?"

Der Flechtemann shut his eyes for a moment, then reopened them with cold resolve. "We be needin' 'em to ready themselves for an ambush on us."

"Wha'?" one of the men said as a general murmur of confusion spread across the assembled camp.

"Before we left, I entrusted Ludomir with the folk unversed in battle. I gave him directives for when the sun's embrace touches those peaks," he gestured eastward, "our comrade shall guide the wagons, loop 'round, and make for the copse of trees to hide."

All at once a general, hushed uproar boiled though out the assembly of rebels, including Yakov. Images of Anna and Dieter circled in his mind, and he stood up, quivering as he confronted the rebel leader.

"Ye be usin' 'em as bait?" Yakov asked in whispered fury. Those same quiet whispers were heard from others assembled who left loved ones with the wagons. Though whispered, the sound posed a problem of discovery if not settled quickly.

"I am," der Flechtemann said trying to justify his decision. Looking at the confused faces of his men, he continued his explanation of his field decision. "I dispatched a fellow afore this very night to spy if the Chain's lot be present. Proceed, let 'em know what ye beheld." He said looking past some of those gathered to a nearby rebel.

A scout sitting nearby against a tree spoke up in a terse voice. "There be a fair bunch o' tough lads, and some drafted souls among 'em. They come across a scruffy bunch all in all, an' their nags ain't much to look at, but their armor be in decent shape, and their blades are solid. The fellas eat hearty, seem to be practicin' sharp, and they've got more scars on their mugs than any measly noble's gang o' dung knights."

"They be present. And they ain't the sort to recklessly rush at," der Flechtemann declared, fixing his gaze on Yakov, his eyes void of any emotion. "Thou art more aware than anyone present of what Petres' crew's capable of."

Yakov was quiet.

"This is what be demanded," der Flechtemann said, looking around at his men as his face softened. "Today, they shall grasp wha' Eugen bore."

As Yakov looked around him, he knew these men would follow der Flechtemann into hell itself. Doubts faded into oblivion, leaving only the purpose and the determination to accomplish it.

***

The clouds mimicked the gray snow on the crown of the hill, casting a dying light on the unfolding scene. The gloom almost choked Yakov as, next to him, the rebels crouched behind the crest, bows at the ready. Earlier their leader, der Flechtemann, carefully positioned his partisans for a flanking attack that would take their foes by surprise. A tense energy thrummed in the air as they waited for the signal to strike.

Then a low, strumming horn broke through the silence, and the first volley of arrows let loose, souring through the white sky like so many bees following their queen to the next hive to build.

Arcing downhill in a deadly curve, the arrows fell like black rain on the mercenary camp, a sprawling, ugly blotch swelling between a curving rise and a curtain of trees. Distant screams tore through the air as desperate stragglers tried to escape into the trees. Yakov imagined being one of them again, distantly, as the arrows tore through the conscripts, leaving red trails on the snow.

His heart pounded in his chest as he watched the battle unfold from his vantage point next to the archers. His grip tightened on the blunt woodsman's axe given him to carry for self-defense, his knuckles white as he fought the urge to wretch.

Arrows continued to soar through the air, their deadly flight guided by skilled hands. He marveled at the rebels' accuracy, their arrows finding their marks with uncanny precision. His eyes flickered between the struggling combatants in the distance, searching for glimpses of familiar faces among the mercenaries. The cries of pain and the rallying shouts deafened him.

Amidst the fray, Yakov's gaze was drawn to a figure at the forefront of the mercenaries—the Chain himself. The man's imposing presence was undeniable, his leathery face twisted by an ugly grin as he led his men in the desperate struggle.

Yakov's jaw tightened, a mixture of apprehension and sheer dread stirring within him at seeing the man. He observed the Chain's calculated strikes, the way the man moved, rallying his forces even in the face of adversity. The Chain's reputation as a ruthless cutthroat was well-deserved, and Yakov knew this battle would be no easy victory.

"Steady!" Petres the Chain roared, laughing madly, his voice carrying above the din of preparations. "Stand yer ground! These wretched rodents shall nay savor a simple conquest 'pon this blasted frost!"

A hushed silence fell over the battlefield as a second horn blew from der Flechtemann's position. High and sharp—a signal ignited the charge. With a unified roar, the rebels surged forward, their arrows flying like deadly rain. Sieghart, at the head of a dozen horses, tore down the hill with a spear raised over his head as he screamed in defiance. The twang of bowstrings, the clash of hooves against the earth, and the thunk of arrows punching through chainmail sang discordantly through the air. Mercenaries fell, their cries of pain mingling with the cries of defiance from both sides. The survivors, still caught off guard by this rear assault, scrambled to respond, hurriedly grabbing shields to lift over their heads. "Shield wall," someone called, but it was far too late.

The mercenaries, already shaken by the sudden attack, were now further disoriented as they tried to face both the rebels charging from the rear and those engaging them head-on. The chaos of battle obscured their vision, making it difficult to discern friend from foe. Again, shields raised in haste proved insufficient as the rebel cavalry bore down upon them. The force of the charge shattered the mercenaries' lines, sending some stumbling, others falling to the ground. The rebels exploited the chaos, and their arrows struck true.

"Shield wall, y'bastards!" again came the Chain's annoyance. "Hold that cursed wall, ye poxed knaves!"

"Release!" came Der Flechtemann's own call, followed by another horn, directing his archers to release another volley of arrows. The mercenaries' formation began to crumble under the relentless barrage, and panic began to set in. With grim satisfaction, Yakov noticed the Chain's lopsided grin now fallen away, his bravado having given way to a stark realization of the dire situation.

The mercenaries, disorganized and demoralized, found themselves pushed back by the unrelenting assault. The archers' arrows continued to rain down upon them, thinning their ranks and sowing further panic. Meanwhile, Sieghart led his cavalry in a swift retreat, regrouping with the main rebel forces, panting as he lifted his bloody spear triumphantly. Their charge struck a decisive blow, creating a rift within the mercenaries' ranks that left them vulnerable. As he rode past, he caught Yakov's eye and grinned, before looking at the other archers.

"Fer every lad we lost!" he roared, and with an answering bout of hoots, the rebels nocked another volley, prepared for der Flechtemann's signal. But here he was himself, der Flechtemann, striding through the trees to stand with his archers.

"Aim for the enemy commander!" he commanded.

"Draw!"

They drew.

"Hold!"

They held.

"Loose!" der Flechtemann roared, and the volley released, heading directly for the column of men where the Chain commanded, astride a black warhorse, his Warhammer slung across his shoulder.

But by luck or some devilish providence, the Chain chose that very moment to ride to relief of another pocket of his men, who seemed at the brink of desertion. Most of the arrows sailed past him harmlessly as he snarled in surprise, fiddling with his shield, an ornate piece emblazoned with a crimson hound. But even as two arrows thudded against its rough surface, a third arrow found its way into his face. There was a gory flash and a screaming Petres fell from his horse, narrowly rolling away from his own horse's hoofs before it trampled him.

But even as a cheer ran through the rebel lines, Yakov watched with horror as the Chain stood up, tearing the arrow form his face with a scream as he ran.

"Retreat, men, ye dogs, ye half-killed comrades!" he screamed as he ran, threatening his cowering soldiers with desperate kicks as he skidded downhill. "Run, bastards!"

Yakov, breathing heavily, turned and grabbed der Flechteman's arm, eyes wide. "Y'have to kill 'im! If he lives…if he…"

Nodding without looking at him, Der Flechtemann gave the order: "Set yer arrows to attack the Chain!" Sharp tips were again raised skyward. The order amplified with a snarl across his poised men.

"Loose!"

Petres the Chain cursed and ran downhill, pulling one of his fleeing men from his palfrey before clambering into the saddle. His bloody face left a red streak on the horse's flank as it rubbed against the steed. Narrowly, the horse avoided the arrows as it charged toward the cover of the trees.

"Hold!" der Flechtemann ordered with a note of frustration in his voice. The archers stopped with mutterings and groans, arrows missing, their aim far too used to striking the mark.

"Nay, there be no chance for him to endure an arrow lodged in his cursed face." Sieg muttered as he dismounted his own horse, walking towards them.

As a terrible coldness gnawed at him Yakov stood in silent thought, *The Chain, that devil! Despite hope, he yet lives*. Yakov shivered at the thought that his worst nightmare still roamed the green earth like the godless, corrupt wretch he was. As his breath shuddered, der Flechtemann gave Yakov an algid look, then turned to face Sieghart.

"Round up some of the lads," der Flechtemann ordered. "Capture as needs capturin' and put any sorry bastard out of his suffering who is too far gone to survive."

Sieg nodded and left, and Yakov looked down at the carnage of the camp, as bloody men dragged themselves, crying like children. A mercenary, leveraging himself against a tree, kicked his legs out wildly as he tried to push through the arrow embedded in his side, life's blood pooling in the soil around him.

Yakov's knees collapsed into the powdery snow, too much to take in as bile rose in his throat. He puked, then looked through the distortion of tears, mercifully blurring his eyes to the horror before him. Near him, der Flechtemann feigned to gag then spat an ugly mass on the ground. Looking back to where Yakov knelt, this strong visage, holding his own phlegm with effort, eyes wooden, nodded his head in the direction of the death and carnage. The rebel leader uttered one short epithet, "This be the bitter fruit of the hunt."

Chapter XVIII: O, Our Father…

"O, our Father, who art in heaven, hallowed be thy name; thy kingdom come; thy will be done…but by what hand? Shall it be the shaking hand of the priest, quivering with golden bands? Shall it be the fat paw of the [landowner]? Or shall it be the [rough] palm of a man as kind as his cruelty, as true as his lies, and as great as his rags…"

-Unknown Monk, circa 1383

The sun began its descent, casting long shadows across the silent snow. The rebels returned to the quiet clearing in the copse where the injured partisans, women, children and elderly camped. Now drifting back, they looked for kin or a place to rest. Archers stretched their bow hands, yawning as they looked at the sky. Meanwhile, Sieghart helped some of his injured cavalrymen find what comfort they could.

Yakov, now finding solace, sat on a weathered log as he cradled a steaming bowl of soup in his hands. The aroma of the stew, concocted by Anna's skilled hands, wafted up to his nose, momentarily pulling him from the memories of the battle that still churned within him. He took a slow sip, the warmth of the broth spreading through him.

As he continued to drink the soup, his thoughts drifted back to the battle. The cries of pain, and the urgency of survival replayed in his mind like a relentless loop. The images of the mercenaries falling, the look of desperation in their eyes, lingered like ghosts at the edge of his consciousness.

A soft rustle of footsteps brought him back to the present. Anna approached, her eyes holding a mix of concern and understanding. She settled beside him, her presence a quiet reassurance he was not alone to grapple with the aftermath of the battle and his own conflicted feelings.

"Look now," she said softly, offering a small piece of bread to accompany the soup. "Ye mustn't let yer strength wane."

Yakov nodded, quietly taking the bread he dipped it into the soup. It tasted like ash to him in his numb state of mind, but the warmth of the food still offered a semblance of comfort—something he desperately needed.

"'Tis over now," Anna said, her voice gentle.

Yakov met her gaze, the weight of years wasted reflected in his eyes. "Be it?"

"How mean ye?"

"I mean," Yakov said slowly, turning stiffly to look at Sieg and the other rebels, "Be it truly done? Cast your gaze 'round, sister. We're the cog in this uprising. A modest cog, true, and mayhaps we'll ne'er even graze the emperor's snout with our deeds—but a rebellion it be, nonetheless. What duke, count, or even baron would grant us to roam unfettered, adrift in fantasies? What plump merchant would abide der Flechtemann's shafts piercing his coffers, 'less the gold flows out 'til naught remains?"

"Ye've met der Flechtemann," Anna said. "He be a great man, aye? Y'believe in him. I see it in yer eyes."

"He used ye and Dieter and a whole encampment of folk unskilled in combat as a lure, he did." Yakov said, raising an eyebrow.

Anna paused and quietly looked at Yakov, then spoke, "Still. Y'do believe in this. Y'believe in the cause."

"I believe…" Yakov said, then chuckled bitterly. "Christ above knows just *what* I believe. Have nay idea myself. I see the reason for these folk to fight, and I see the evilness of the times. But t'believe…that be t'believe in the possibility of success of thy belief…or something like that," Yakov trailed off, suddenly aware of Anna's uncomprehending gaze.

Anna quizzically shook her head. "Ye weave words like riddles at times, young Yakov." She raised her head and looking into his eyes, "Yet nay, you're grown past the 'little' now. Y've glimpsed more of this world than yer sister; perchance even more than 'tis good for ye—and thus…" she hesitated for a long pause. "What d'ye think we should do? D'ye want to leave this camp?"

Yakov thought about it, conflicted. He looked at the faces of his new comrades, battle-hardened and determined, each one carrying their own burdens. Secure in the knowledge the cause they embraced was undeniably just, and Yakov envied in them their certainty.

"Leavin' this camp could rightly be wise, aye," came a voice, and they turned with some surprise to see Dieter standing quietly nearby. "Aye, but what if 'tis the wrong path, huh? Stickin' 'round means more clashes, more spillin' o'blood, more goodbyes, and more of the damn unknown. Yet, listen to Anna, and it seems there ain't naught else awaitin' us beyond these walls."

As Yakov mulled it over, he became aware of another presence. He looked up to see der Flechtemann walking towards them with his horse in tow, his head slightly bowed, his quiver swinging in rhythm to his practiced, focused gait. Sieg followed him, shouting orders to rebels along the way. For the first time, Yakov noticed how truly tall the rebel leader was—Yakov was of a tall build himself, but der Flechtemann's lanky frame and slight hunch reminded Yakov of an old magician from some children's tale, missing only a long flowing beard. The image of der Flechtemann's gigantic head and neckless countenance; however, were illusions of the thickness of his mien which grew unkempt in every direction. He often reminded Yakov more of the trolls of legend. Der Flechtemann's stature and gait being somewhat familiar strangely reminded Yakov of something in his past, though he couldn't quite place it.

"I hope t'find ye all well," der Flechtemann said, looking at the siblings. Anna nodded, unsure of how to act before the famed leader of the cause. She rose to attempt a clumsy curtsy, then thought better of doing so and sat back down nervously. Yakov remained still, looking into the face of the man before him.

"Ye be leavin'," Yakov observed.

"Aye," der Flechtemann said, sighing. "Off on a fool's journey, we be. The coming fortnight we'll strive to trace the Chain's path." Eyeing Yakov with an offhand look, he continued, "I'll aim to send another arrow his way; mayhaps this time 'twill find its mark 'twixt those monstrous brows of his."

"And if y'don't find 'em?" Yakov quarried.

"Then I'll set my sights on scoutin' the southern lands," der Flecthemann said, his tone resolute. "Methinks, if the Chain finds his way back hale and hearty to that accursed abbot of his, he'll come down on us like a swarm of devil's-teeth from the north, leadin' an army thrice our size. 'Fore that dark hour, we must gather more archers under our banner, and secure a steady, secure path southward."

Yakov nodded, shuddering as he imagined Petres's fury. He knew enough to know the Chain to be a vengeful man. Beneath the mask of arbitrary sadism, lay an obsessive madman who would stop at nothing to nail der Flechtemann's hide to a tree.

"What of ye?" der Flechtemann asked unexpectedly of the siblings. "I know yer homestead be lost or sold, yer Uncle Karl spent yer earnin's, so y'have nowhere to be— mayhaps if ye'd rather be at peace than part of this battle, we can leave ye at a village with some coin. Nay any man fights here tha' does not want."

Yakov looked at him and said nothing, frowning. Sieghart's eyes flicked in alarm from Yakov to Anna, clearly worried to lose her.

"I…we…"Anna stammered, caught off guard as Yakov didn't reply. "Aye, we be just thinkin' about tha'."

Der Flechtemann nodded. "Give the word to young Sieghart yer decidin', and he'll make it so."

Anna looked at Sieg helplessly as der Flechtemann walked past, his horse's hoof-falls muffled in the grass. Just then, however, Yakov suddenly spoke.

"Anna," Yakov said quietly. "Did ye ever mention Uncle Karl's name to 'em?"

Der Flechtemann froze.

"I—what?" Anna asked confused.

"He said 'yer *Uncle Karl* spent yer earnin's'. Did ye ever tell 'em Karl's name?"

"Nay," Anna said, confused now as well. "But…"

Turning to the rebel leader Yakov asked, "How did ye know his name?" He continued to stare at der Flechtemann's back with narrowed eyes. There was still no reply.

"Yakov don't go actin'—so stiff," Anna muttered, her cheeks all aflush. "Ain't he the one who kept us safe and sound after all? Even Sieg lingered at the cottage and shared words with Karl, so there must've been some sharin'…"

Yakov looked at Sieghart. "Did y'tell der Flechtemann our uncle's name?"

Sieg looked from face to face hesitantly, entirely unsure about whatever was going on. His gaze fell on his leader's immobile back, as if waiting for an order to speak or not speak. No order came.

"Nay, I didn't," Sieg finally said in an uncertain tone. "Truth be told, I plumb forgot 'is name soon as we left the homestead."

Dieter and Anna looked at Yakov. Curiously their gaze, too, fell on the rebel leader, who was still frozen with his back to them. His horse whinnied softly, as if picking up on his unease.

"How did ye know his name?" Yakov asked him flatly, his body coiled. He did not know what troublesome story lay amiss here, but something uncanny lurked in the electricity of the moment. His hand slowly curled around the gnarled haft of the ax resting next to him.

Then, der Flechtemann sighed, turning his gaze to the night sky. Piercing pin lights of stars punctured the deep, cold blue, around him and gleamed like watchful eyes in the dark. The clouds were still touched with a profound, nostalgic pink, against which his silhouette reminded those gathered bringing back to life a halo of memories. The campfire crackled not too far away. Its distant wash of red light created a pool of shadow at his feet.

Der Flechtemann looked down at his shadow reflecting on what to say next.

"Karl was always a damned fool," he said, his voice grim.

Stunned silence pervaded the scene. The knuckles of Yakov's hand turned white with the strangle grip he held on to the haft of his weapon. "Who be ye?" he demanded to know.

The rebel leader turned, his face strained with the weight of what he must admit, desperately trying to maintain his impassive mask. For the first time Yakov looked at the man before him—this passionate emissary for good. Focusing on the visage of this face, a growing realization dawned on the young partisan. Under the fur of der Flechtemann's beard, Yakov could imagine the hidden sharpness of the man's jaw. As this proud partisan leader thought for another moment, he swallowed in resolution, and Yakov noticed a prominent movement of der Flechtemann's neck, familiar yet elusive. Now taking in the full countenance of the leader's face, Yakov's gaze locked deep into the pale yet brilliant green eyes piercing him with their stare. Finally, in an awakening mind's image, a young soldier now a man, felt time pulling him backward to his childhood, before time itself. The birth of a new beginning shoved him peering into a mirror where the future of his own face now aged over the many years hence.

Der Flechtemann gazed beyond Yakov's shoulder. His emotions rebuilding the wall around which he placed past years, and stowing those memories away, responded, "I'm your father."

Anna gasped. Her eyes wide. Her hands shook, and in an instant, she was a blur. She charged ahead with wild eyes, shrieking wordlessly. The men around the campfire startled by the ripping apart of the quiet in the dark night. Sieg immediately leaped forward to restrain Anna as she wailed, afraid she might hurt someone with her flailing hands and nails.

"Aye, lend a hand, Yakov!" Sieg grunted, trying to hold Anna off. No response came. He turned his head to call again. "Yakov?"

Yakov sat in place, ghostly pale, expression glazed over. Not too far away, Dieter stood with a stunned look on his face. Der Flechtemann stood resolutely in their midst without reaction, consciously not looking in Anna's direction.

"Hans," Yakov muttered, his eyes distant. "Yer name be Hans Symon. Ye were…"

"Fletcher," said der Flechtemann, his voice tired. "Aye, craftsman of wood; skilled worker of many tasks. Anything that kept the coin comin', kept the homestead runnin'."

Anna's struggles subsided somewhat, her face still a mask of shock and anger, tears streaming down her flushed cheeks. She remained in Sieg's grasp, trembling, before der Flechtemann. Her voice quivered as she spoke, "Y'left us. Y'left your own family. Can ye… can ye even *imagine* what we went through?"

"Aye, I can," der Flechtemann said in a stony voice. "Ye went through what every commoner in this damn empire goes through. Ye went through the same sufferin' as meself, the same sufferin' every man, woman, and child of common blood goes through. What ye went through is the very thing I fight against."

"Y'left yer own children!" Anna retorted, shaking.

Der Flechtemann's weathered face showed a flicker of regret as he met Anna's gaze. "Aye, I did what I must…The cause be righteous. 'Twas to be that moment or nevermore."

Anna clenched her fists, tears welling in her eyes. "*The cause?* Y'chose a cause over us. Over yer own children."

Yakov finally stirred from the foggy daze presented in the mind between anger and chagrin. His raspy voice filled with an abundant mixture of confusion and bitterness. "And while ye fought for…this *cause*, we suffered. Mother…y'don't even know what she went through, do ye? Did y'know she stopped movin'? Stopped talkin'? Stopped all, but for breathin'? That she couldn't…she couldn't…" He trailed off, and for a moment his mother's vacant face appeared to him through time, her view of him unseeing. His eyes grew wet, and a single, warm tear trickled down his face.

"Ye left us with Karl, who stood upon us, bottle in hand," Anna said, still quivering with anger, now pointing a shaking finger at Yakov's teary face. "And *he,* yer eldest son," she continued with accusation, "…marched as the devil's pawn in war. He bein' sent to fight battles he'd nay a stake in and be blooded in battle while serving those nobles ye hate so much. If ye ha' just *been there,"* she pleaded. "…he would ne'er have gone to Helmstedt, nay ne'er…"

She broke into sobs again. Sieg reached for her once more, pulling her close, uncertain about what to do. Dieter stood with a stunned expression, his hesitant hand on his brother's shoulder as Yakov looked off into nothing frustrated with dismay.

Der Flechtemann's eyes remained fixed on the ground, his silence a heavy acknowledgment of his children's pain. The crackling of the campfire punctuated the quiet of the night trying to dispel the tense atmosphere.

"The cause be right and true." He declared at last, his words burdened by the weight of years filled with yearning and rue. "The tyranny we endure, the sufferin' of the common folk, the tax upon tax upon unlawful tax—I lived through it. I lived through things ye can't imagine. I…knew not of your dear mother, and I thought too kindly of Karl, 'tis true. These be knowingly but a few of my transgressions; yet, whether ye grant me pardon or withhold it, be in yer hands." He looked up at Anna, his even gaze pierced deeply into her angry face for some recognition of understanding. "Aye, someone needed to rise and take a stand."

Anna's fury battled with the remnants of a daughter's longing for her father. She turned away, wiping tears from her cheeks. Dieter, still processing the revelation, watched the scene with wide eyes.

"Dieter, lad," der Flechtemann said, addressing his youngest son. "I ne'er saw yer birth. If I'd stayed t'see ye born, I may ne'er ha' left. Understand, I…ne'er wanted ye to endure what y'did." He paused, then continued with quiet resolve, "None of ye. But I couldn't stay, not while the world be as 'twas."

Yakov, with a deep melancholy in his eyes, finally looked at der Flechtemann and spoke. "As y'said—y'made yer choice--Hans." He reasoned, calling his father by name, distance in his voice. "Nay, seems there ain't much of a choice left now, do there?"

Der Flechtemann shook his head quietly. The campfire crackled on, casting flickering shadows on the faces of the fractured family. The wounds of the past were laid bare, and yet the fire of his conviction still burned in der Flechtemann's jaded eyes.

Anna recognized those eyes, now. She recognized the face, once smiling, though always worry-creased, looking down at her as he presented her with a wooden doll, he carved especially for her. She loved the gift of love her father painstakingly etched into her doll. Uncle Karl, though, stole it one day to sell for yet another bottle. The sot, she remembered, drunk as usual, *tried to justify himself, saying a woman of thirteen summers, nearly grown had no business with toys*. That night, Anna steeped in tears wished her father would return. The next day, however, Anna realized her childhood now passed beyond her grasp never to return.

Her once-father now stood before her, unrecognizable, like a creature from a half-forgotten fable, with a ready quiver and gray hair. At his side, a finger twitched—the only sign that he was in any distress.

Around the campfire, the rebels watched in solemn silence, bearing witness to the painful reunion. The men, used as they were to talking amidst themselves freely, hushed now, increasingly aware of the circumstances. The crackling flames of the campfire seemed to echo their burning questions, but no tongue rose in that moment, silenced by the sheer weight of the confrontation before them.

Anna, her voice filled with abject bitterness, looked with revolt once more at her father. "Y'left yer family, and made another out of yer cause. Now y'stand here, and…I wish I could hate ye. I wish I could hate this damn cause." Seeking to be alone, she broke free of Sieg's protective arms and stomped passionately away from camp, her face buried in the private crook of her arm.

Sieg looked to Yakov and Dieter as if asking for leave to go after her. "Aye, go on," said Yakov, nodding stiffly. "Take care of her."

Sieghart gave him a grateful look and jogged away. "Anna, wait!" he pleaded, following her away from the firelight.

Yakov took a deep breath and looked at his father. The two hollow men looked at each other, understanding but not understanding, the same and yet entirely different, joined in their pain, yet knowing two entirely different worlds of suffering. Yakov's face was a mask, and behind the mask a child still cried out for his father. In similarity, behind der Flechtemann's determined eyes, a father longed to embrace his son, but they simply stood, unmoving.

"Y'better go," Yakov said finally. "Scouts rode ahead earlier, aye?"

The rebel leader nodded. "Have t'regroup with them soon."

"Best get to it."

"Aye," der Flechtemann said, clearing his throat as he mounted his horse, patting its neck absently as he looked at Yakov. He hesitated for a moment.

"'Bout yer mother, I…" he paused, and couldn't seem to find the words he needed. Finally, he said, "Jus' take care o' yer sister."

Yakov nodded, saying nothing. Der Flechtemann gave him a final look, as if begging him to understand—then, taking a lighted torch from one of the men nearby, rode away in a steady canter. Yakov sat quietly as Dieter settled next to him, listening to the hoof-falls fade away. The rest of the rebels offered them sympathetic looks and hesitant nods, but no idea came as to what to say. If they talked about the incident, they did so in hushed voices, out of earshot.

"He be gone?" Yakov asked evenly.

Dieter turned around to check. "Aye, he's gone off."

Yakov nodded, then managed a dry chuckle at Dieter's solemn expression. "Aye. Must be strangest for ye, a fresh brother and a father within a single year's span, that be a turn of fortune, indeed."

"It's a strange life, aye," Dieter said with an amused look. "But as long as the heavens don't give me another Anna, all is well."

"Another Ann?" Yakov mused, arching his brows. "Two of our Annas would be a rebellion all on their lonesome—enough to send these folks scurryin' for work elsewhere."

The brothers chuckled together, trying not to think about much. Inch by inch, they came closer to the fire as the night grew cold, until they sat amidst the other rebels, the rationed beer passed from one welcoming hand to another. Soon, Dieter, not being allowed to drink under Anna's usual presence, sat red-faced and coughing. For his part, Yakov slapped his brother on the back as he himself took slow, measured sips of the stout liquor, his eyes looking into the fire with thoughts of many things he could not put into words. Not too far from camp, Anna lay in Sieg's arms, still crying as he calmed her, his gentle hand stroking her hair.

Still staring into the fire, Yakov's mind drifted to a faraway place. Despite himself, he thought about his father. *Somewhere in the distant darkness, perhaps der Flechtemann stopped his horse long enough to take another wistful glance back at the camp where his children were trying not to think of him. Perhaps he longed to be with them, laughing under the night sky, truly a father and not a rebel, not a savior, not a hope, not a warrior—just a father.*

Or perhaps, he rode on into the night, his heart walled against his own longing, with the resigned eyes of a man marching off into war.

Now quite aware a shadow of a great man and a great cause dwelled within his mind never to be removed, Yakov paused and sighed. *No, the son may never know the true*

*thoughts of his father. But much to his dismay, in the shadow,
he found the resting place for Hans Symon who died years
ago so der Flechtemann might live.*

Chapter XIX: Epilogue

-Brother Jakob, circa 1384

Michael rubbed the bridge of his nose, another all-nighter spent as he and James read in the dim light of this room, returning again and again to this monk's cloister within an old Abby. He leaned back and blinked to encourage tears to wet the dryness in his tired eyes. Across from him, James propped himself against a chair back, a thin line pursed his mouth, a far-off stare morphed his face with some new idea awkwardly brewing. As Michael watched, now slapping his own face to chase away sleep, he marveled at James intensity.

Weeks flew by as they parsed through documents, creating a wholly chronological account. Long hours of reviewing and interpreting encouraged the pair to continue to look. The more they looked the more exciting the adventure to discover the past became. Though the story told in the pages was very much the story of a single life—Yakov Symon's life—the writer wrote in a strange flow over many years, moving from thought to thought like a butterfly through a garden. The combined expertise of both James and Michael proved invaluable at skimming through the old

German passages, as the author switched between German and Latin at random, puzzling intervals.

"Well, that was…something," James managed. Stretching, he looked at the clock—4AM. They sat in the hotel room in which Michael stayed, all glossy wood and white drapery.

"It was," Michael said, shaking his head. "The implication that this der Flechtemann person in reality was none other than Yaklov's father created a rather unusual reveal…facts can be stranger than fiction sometimes."

James nodded, then appeared to notice something odd. He squinted at the page and his eyebrows slowly raised as a thought entered his mind and began to grow. Michael could almost cogs turning.

"What is it?" Michael asked, leaning forward and wincing as a spasm of backpain surged in his spine from sitting around on a hard seat all day. "Oh, that hurt." He grimaced again as he stretched.

"Look at this," James said, pointing at a scribble in the inner margin of the last page of the document. Faded and barely perceptible, as though scrawled with an almost-dry quill, the visible scrapings suggest a name.

"Brother…Ja…" Michael read aloud, squinting.

"Jakob. Brother Jakob," James said, looking intently at Michael, almost expectantly.

In a sudden flash of thought as if two worlds collided in the universe, everything Michael and James struggled to piece together seemed to click into place. "Jakob," Michael said slowly, eyes widening. "*Yakov*. So the author of this book is…?"

"The Yakov Symon in the story," James said, nodding with excitement. The last sleepless night or two faded asway. "Both names come from the same Hebrew root, true?"

"*Akev*, I think," Michael said, frowning. "But this doesn't make sense. Why did Yakov change his name? And why would he ever become a Benedictine monk, especially since he thought he may be Jewish…at least the lineage of the name would imply so? Perhaps to hide his faith? And there is the spelling of the last name, Symon, a Prussian name or at the least of Polish origin. At that time in history Germanic people and the Prussians were not on the best of terms." Michael added.

"Also, linguistically, the manuscript was very vague whenever Yakov mentioned god," James mused. "Perhaps to mask whether he was catholic or Jewish? Or was he simply a convert trying to find a simpler escape from conflicts of his day?"

"But for an illiterate youth who fought alongside mercenaries, ended up in a camp of rebels, finally turning to their cause,…" Michael shook his head in wonder. "…to become a *monk*, of all things…that's some story."

James grinned. "Sure is. So—did we find what you were looking for, my friend? This story that is?"

Michael smiled. "It's a start, and a promising one. I see you're excited about this too."

"Of course," James said, reverently touching the ancient pages. "I can't overstate how incredible this opportunity is. Honestly, I want to just keep going."

Michael laughed. "As wonderful as that would be, humans do still need sleep, last I checked. Go get some rest. The manuscript's not going anywhere."

James nodded, and after Michael and he shook hands, he left with his reference books and reading tools. Michael packed the manuscript back into its ancient box with reverential care, thinking about Yakov and der Flechtemann, and the bond the father and son never had. This lack of trust between father and son was a sad thing, he reflected. Pausing for a moment, he looked in his room's mirror. Thoughts of him and his own son came to mind.

Picking up his mobile, he scrolled until his son's profile picture cropped up. He found a couple pictures of his Gary and Vivian grinning at the camera. Michael smiled back at the screen before placing his called.

"Hey dad," came Gary's voice, sounding surprised. "Everything alright? What time is it there?"

Michael chuckled. "Late enough to be early. Just missed you, son. How are things back home?"

Michael could almost hear Gary rolling his eyes. "Dad, you're the one vacationing in Europe. How are things back in the Old World?"

Michael laughed, and as they talked, he was thankful. Thankful to have a loving son, grateful for his entire family, grateful for the chance life gave him, and grateful, again, and always, to Rachel. A choice was made between his wife and him long before cancer took her, a choice to seek out this adventure together. After her death Michael shut down for a time to heal. Now, however, to fulfill their dreams, the choice became clear to honor his wife's request: 'to go.' Now, all those discoveries which haf happened were revelations, and all that would happen would be a long line of welcome discoveries. Michael would become the seeker, following the path to its end.

www.ingramcontent.com/pod-product-compliance
Lightning Source LLC
Chambersburg PA
CBHW060347310726

48976CB00003B/751